'Who are you?' Beoc asked quietly.

The young woman lay back in the water and Beoc caught a glimpse of a green-gold tail undulating gently beneath the surface of the water. 'I am Liban,' she said slowly, 'once daughter of Necca and Ebblue, who walked this land some three hundred and more of your years ago.'

'Necca and Ebblue! But they are myths; this lake is called after Necca... Lough Necca.'

'He was my father.' The mermaid smiled at the young monk's confusion. 'Oh, but do not think I always wore this form; listen and I will tell you my tale . . .'

# Irish Folk and Fairy Tales Volume 3

**MICHAEL SCOTT**

SPHERE BOOKS LIMITED
30–32 Gray's Inn Road, London WC1X 8JL

First published in Great Britain by
Sphere Books Ltd 1984
Copyright © 1984 by Michael Scott

TRADE
MARK

Set in Garamond

Printed and bound in Great Britain by
Collins, Glasgow

For Anna,
*hoc opus, hic labor est.*

# *Contents*

# Chapter One

# ARRIVAL

The sorceress held up the goat's steaming entrails in the fresh morning air; drops of thick dark blood spattered her face and breasts and ran down her slender arms, but she ignored them as she sought to decipher the signs.

The morning sun broke through the greying clouds behind her and ran slickly along the glistening ropes, tingeing them with pink, making them faintly translucent. And in the intricate whorls and creases the small, sallow-skinned woman read the future, divining the trends, the possibilities and the probabilities.

The sorceress nodded slowly and carefully dropped the entrails into the brazier before her. The flesh hissed and spat and tainted the fresh salt air with the smell of burning meat. Sinde then bowed to the four cardinal points and silently offered the remains of the animal to her own dark gods. She then stepped back and indicated that her servants might toss the carcass into the purifying flames. The small woman accepted a cloth from an acolyte and wiped away most of the blood before walking across the smooth sandy beach to where her mistress sat on a low flat stone at the foot of the cliffs with Cipine, Trayim and Ain her principal advisors. The four women looked up as the sorceress joined them.

'Well?' Caesir asked quietly, her huge dark eyes wide and concerned.

'It is as I predicted,' Sinde whispered, 'the waters rise slowly but surely; the goddess approaches with each passing day...'

Unconsciously the four women glanced skywards, where the huge disc of the moon hung low in the sky, its broken irregular features clearly visible even though the sun now rode high in the sky. For the past few seasons, the great white goddess had been steadily approaching the domain of man, as if the goddess herself wished to walk his world.

And for the past few seasons – especially at the turn of the year – the tides had been getting higher and higher and much of the lowlands along the banks of the Nile had been submerged with great loss of life and crops. Even Caesir's own island, Meroe, was now much reduced in size, and it was no longer possible to walk across to the mainland at low tide.

'What will happen?' Cipine, a huge woman clad only in a loin cloth and gold bangles, asked.

Sinde shrugged. 'If the waters continue to rise as the goddess nears, then I fear she will soon be ruling a land of waves only.'

The red-haired northerner grimaced. She was used to fighting tangible foes; the elements were something beyond her control – and for the first time in her long and bloody career she was frightened. 'What can we do?' she asked quietly.

Before Sinde could answer, Caesir held up her slim hand, her pointed nails glistening in the sunlight. 'If the goddess comes to earth,' she asked the sorceress, 'where will she rest?'

Sinde considered, and then she pointed to the south and west. 'In the waves, many days hence.'

'Are we not safe then?' Ain, the tall dark-skinned, curly-haired warrior from the lush rainforests to the far south, asked.

'Nowhere will be safe,' Sinde said quietly. 'When the

2

goddess lands, she will create a wave that will sweep all before it; those in the valleys and,' – she smiled bitterly – 'on the islands, will be called to their gods.'

Ain frowned, and then her startlingly white teeth flashed in a smile. 'If the wave is coming in from the west, could we not flee into the east?' She glanced across at the princess. 'There is no dishonour in fleeing before a stronger enemy. There is a saying in my homeland: "Flee before a hungry beast, for he is easily taken when he has eaten his fill."'

Caesir nodded, sunlight gliding down her sleek black hair. 'No, there is no dishonour in fleeing; but is there anywhere to flee to?' She leaned forward and stared intently at the sorceress. 'What land is there to the west? What is the last land before the Emptiness?'

Sinde laughed gently, the sound no louder than the sighing of the wind. 'I have told you before,' she whispered, 'there is no emptiness; this world is like a fruit, a ball, it is round.'

Cipine laughed good-naturedly. 'Aye, so you've said, and some day we'll sail to the very edge of the world and you can tell me again as we stand and watch the waters boil over into the Nothingness.'

The tiny easterner smiled and bowed. 'Yes, some day we will.'

Caesir turned back to the sorceress. 'But is there land to the west?' she persisted.

Sinde knelt on the warm golden sands and drove her hands deep into the smooth grains. Her dark eyes closed and she spoke aloud in the sibilant, whispering language of her race. The air began to tingle and the fresh salt odour was replaced with a harsh metallic taste. And slowly the sand began to shift and flow. Strange arcane patterns etched themselves into the sand at the women's feet; images formed, some reminiscent of beasts, some of men and, even more disturbing, some that were a mixture of both, like Caesir's animal-headed, man-bodied gods.

3

And then an abstract pattern formed, a strange irregular circle, cut almost in half by a large depression. The sand continued to flow and suddenly Cipine leaned forward and pointed with her short blunt fingers.

'It is a map!'

Caesir fell to her knees in the sand. 'Yes, a map; I have seen my father use something similar ... and we are here!' She pointed to the lower right-hand corner of the design.

The sorceress nodded. 'And now let us see what will happen when the waters come,' she said. She bent her head and murmured again in her own tongue, and once again the sand shifted and flowed. This time, however, the movement began on the right-hand side, and swept slowly across the design, obliterating most of it, leaving only tiny sections untouched; only in the far left-hand corner did any semblance of the original design remain. Sinde sighed and sat back on her heels.

Caesir stood, her long gown whispering as it settled about her tall, slim figure. 'We must flee into the west then,' she said quietly, almost to herself. She stared down the beach to where the muddy waters of the Nile lapped at the brazier and the smoking remains of the sacrifice. Her eyes traced the shoreline, noticing where the waters had risen over the past few seasons, and reclaimed the land to itself. Once the island had been longer ... twice as long as it was broad ... but not now. The princess glanced up into the heavens; soon the goddess would descend, and then the waves would sweep in from the west ... She shuddered. Few would survive the goddess' coming.

Caesir turned back to the women. 'You must gather your forces; Cipine, choose sixteen of your bravest warriors; Ain, the same number of your best trackers and hunters; Trayim, fifteen of your craftswomen. They must be ready to leave within the five-day, they must be prepared to leave their families, friends and possessions ... and above all, they must be sworn to secrecy.'

4

Cipine stood, towering over the princess by more than a head, and almost twice as broad. 'Just over fifty of us and yourself then... is that all?'

Caesir paused and then smiled. 'Fintane will come with me...'

Cipine laughed gruffly. 'I thought he might.'

'My father, Bith, will accompany us also,' the princess added.

'We will need a pilot,' Trayim suggested quietly, 'even just to navigate us up the river.'

Caesir nodded. 'Any suggestions?'

'A countryman of mine, Landra,' Ain said. 'His skill with crafts and vessels of all descriptions is second to none.'

'I have heard of him,' Cipine agreed, 'he is good.'

'Approach him then,' Caesir said absently, looking down the beach, 'swear him to secrecy and then tell him a little... but only as much as he needs to know.'

'And if he refuses to come?' Ain asked with a slight smile.

Caesir looked around, her eyes wide with surprise. 'Then kill him, of course.'


Caesir stood beside Sinde in the prow of the long low ship. White water washed in over the jutting prow and darkened their heavy sealskin cloaks. The princess shivered as the chill soaked through to her bones. 'And where are we now?' she asked the sorceress. 'Surely we have neared the end of our journey?'

The small easterner nodded briefly, the movement lost as the frail craft rocked in the treacherous cross-currents that struck amidships. 'Soon,' she shouted above the crash of the waves, 'soon.'

They had been at sea for nearly forty days now, and, curiously, it had taken them far longer to travel the winding length of the rising waters of the Nile than it had to sail across the tideless Middle Sea, out through the Gates onto the endless Western Ocean. They had struck north then, and the weather had quickly turned colder and wetter and the seas rougher.

The princess glanced across to her right. For the past few days they had been following the coast, but this had now disappeared beneath a covering of low grey cloud. 'What of the lands to the far east?' she asked Sinde.

The sorceress shook her head. 'Lost beneath the waves. Most of the lowlands are even now awash; the mountains and hilly areas remain untouched as yet ... but the water is still rising. It will soon reach your land.'

Caesir stared back into the east, her mind's eye seeing past the grey clouds and slate coloured sea, seeing her homeland once again, trying to imagine the ancient civilisation, the palaces, the cities and their teeming inhabitants of many colours. And then she saw the wall of water crashing down and racing inwards sweeping all before it ...

The Nile folk were used to floods, they probably wouldn't even take any special precautions; would disregard the rumours that were trotted out every season about huge walls of water sweeping up the Nile; would carry on regardless; would live and laugh and love; would die ...

'Land,' Sinde said quietly.

The island rose out from the water like a heavy cloud, almost indistinguishable from the sea and sky. From a distance all they could see was barren grey rock, with no sign of either vegetation or wildlife. Even as they neared, and the island took on shape and definition, they could see that nothing moved on the rocky beach, no seabirds called in the air above the island or nested in the cliffs, and no greenery broke the drab greyness.

'That's all?' the princess asked quietly, her voice almost lost in the roar of the waves. 'Are you sure this is the island?'

'Beyond this point there is nothing but water; it would take a season or more to reach the Land Across the Waves.'

Caesir shook her head, disappointment evident in her face and eyes. 'But to have come so far... for this!'

'It is not overlarge,' Sinde agreed, 'but then, we shall not be using it for long,' she added cryptically, and turned away before Caesir could question her further.

The sea around the island was treacherous with shifting cross-currents and Landra struggled with the much battered reed and wattle vessel, bringing it through the jagged rocks and reefs that seemed almost to guard the isle. A spearlike splinter of rock rose up through the current, threatening to split the vessel in two, but a sudden wave carried them up and over the stone, dropping them down into a watery hollow. The abrupt blow sent Caesir tumbling backwards and she slid across the smooth deck towards the edge, her fingernails catching and breaking in the woven reeds.

Cipine shouted in alarm and threw herself forward, but the boat tipped, spilling her to one side, throwing her away from the princess. And then Fintane caught at Caesir's flailing hand. The boat lurched, climbing upwards, knocking him to the deck. His fingers scrabbled along the reeds before catching and he hung there as the craft angled upwards, clinging desperately to the deck with one hand and the princess with the other. Cipine released her grip on the deck and allowed the angle of the craft to send her rolling across to the couple. She grabbed Fintane's foot and held on while the craft righted itself. Ain also threw herself forward and caught a handful of Caesir's cloak, hauling her back from the foaming waves.

Landra the pilot shouted a warning and there were screams of terror as a huge wall of water bore down on them. The massive southerner leaned against the tiller, his muscles bulging as he attempted to wrench the craft to one side.

The boat rose up and seemed to hang momentarily before plunging into the trough. Ain crawled across Caesir and Fintane, covering them with her body, and Cipine anchored

7

herself as best she could to the deck and held on to the southerner. The craft rose and fell again – and this time a rock wall flashed by on the right-hand side, sheering off the oars, scraping the side of the craft. Luckily the oarswomen knew by now when to leave the oars and tie themselves to their benches, and the splintering wood did little damage. The craft was thrown forward, stone scraped briefly along the underside and then the rocks ripped up through it, disembowelling the frail craft... but the momentum of the waves carried it forward and up onto the beach.

The morning dawned bright but chill. Caesir gently disentangled herself from Fintane's arms and crawled out from under the thick wool and hide blanket. She could hear the crackle of burning wood and the aromatic odour perfumed the salt-rich air. She passed two of Cipine's warrior women standing guard in the mouth of the large cave. She had to admire them for their courage and stamina: they had gone through what she had – and more probably – and had then been forced to stand duty for what remained of the evening and through the night.

She found Cipine and Ain standing around a huge fire built amongst the rocks. Wood crackled and sparks spiralled skywards as the northerner added more wood... which, Caesir suddenly realised, was part of their craft. The two women seemed almost unnaturally cheerful considering that they were now marooned on a tiny island at the very edge of the world.

Sinde and Trayim glided silently out from one of the smaller caves and daintily picked their way down the rough beach to the fire. Caesir watched them; from the distance they were almost indistinguishable, they were country-women of the same height and build, with the same racial characteristics: high thin features, slanting eyes, fine hair.

8

They were friends, close friends ... and possibily more than that.

Caesir turned to the sorceress. 'Are we safe here?'

The easterner considered before answering. 'This is the most distant western island from the mainland,' she said slowly, her voice almost lost against the hiss of the surf on the shore. 'Here we will be safe, the rising waters will spend themselves on the continent and be swallowed in the vastness of the ocean. However,' she added with a slight smile, 'it might be wiser to move to the high ground for the next few days ...'

Cipine laughed. 'I've not yet met a magic man or witch who didn't cover themselves in every way.'

'But can we get off this island?' Ain asked.

The sorceress shook her head. 'No.'

'Ssso ...' Caesir looked down the beach to where a small group of women were scouring amongst the stones for driftwood and other sea wreckage, 'here we remain. This is our new home; what is it like, I wonder?' She looked across the leaping flames at Cipine.

The northern mercenary nodded. 'The island is oblong as far as I can see. From up there' – she pointed up towards the cliffs – 'I can see a few rivers, at least one small lake, young trees, grasses.'

Caesir nodded and looked at Ain.

The southerner shivered slightly with the cold and shook her head. 'I can see no signs of habitation ... there are some beast marks, small creatures, and not many at that.'

Trayim the Craftswoman added. 'It would be difficult – if not impossible – to build dwellings of any kind from the trees or grasses. The soil is hard, not suitable for growing, and it is neither rich enough nor of the proper quality to fashion pots and other vessels.'

Caesir turned back to the sorceress.

'What you have been told is true enough. But this island is

rich enough to support us all. Some creatures, little better than beasts, live in the caves on the eastern shores. Further north, livestock is plentiful and the seas about these shores are rich and swarming. I can . . . induce the trees to grow and the grasses to thicken.'

Caesir nodded.

'And now I think we should discuss the problem of breeding,' Trayim said quietly. 'If we are to remain on this island for the rest of our days, surely we should see to it that our children inherit it?'

'There are some fifty women,' Caesir said slowly, 'and three men.'

'And one of them is an old man,' Ain added.

'He is still virile,' Caesir said.

'But for how long?' Trayim asked. 'He is an old man, near the end of his days.'

'Surely it is too soon to be thinking of children?' Caesir asked.

Sinde shook her head. 'Death will soon walk amongst us.'

Caesir turned back to the craftswoman. 'What would you suggest?'

'If we divide the women into three groups,' Trayim said slowly, 'one group to each man. Put some of Cipine's warriors, Ain's hunters and my craftswomen into each group; hopefully, by the end of the season most of the women will be with child. In twelve or fifteen years we can start breeding between the three groups. In our lifetime we could see a strong community growing up.'

'But we need land,' Ain protested. 'At the moment the island can feed us . . . but when children start coming along, that will both decrease the number of hunters and farmers and at the same time increase the number of mouths to feed.'

Sinde looked up from the flames of the fire. 'I can push back the sea and increase the land,' she said.

Caesir sighed. 'Then it only remains for us to divide the

10

women. I will go with Fintane, of course; Ain, will you take your countryman, Landra? And that leaves my father to you, Cipine.' She paused and added, 'Try not to kill him, will you?'

The mercenary grimaced. 'I'll do my best.'

'I understand you need to remain apart from men,' the princess said to the sorceress.

'My magic depends on it,' Sinde said.

'And for that reason also I have excluded you, Trayim. You will remain with Sinde, and ensure that she wants for nothing. We need her powers now as never before.'

The craftswoman bowed silently.

Caesir turned back to Cipine and Ain. 'If you could send out hunting parties today, perhaps we could sort out the groups and set off within the next few days?'

Ain grimaced, her teeth startlingly white against the blackness of her face. 'It's already been done.'

Stones and pebbles clattered down the beach as Fintane stumbled out from the cave, blinking in the morning sunlight. Caesir looked up at him, and then turned back to the group gathered around the fire. 'Until the hunting parties return then?'

The four women nodded and slowly drifted away from the fire. Cipine and Ain wandered down the beach, lost in conversation; for two women from wildly differing cultures and climates they found much in common. Sinde and Trayim turned and climbed back up the beach towards one of the smaller caves, their arms slowly encircling each other's waist. Caesir remained by the fire waiting for Fintane to join her, watching the remains of their vessel turn to black ash.

And above them on the cliffs, flat, yellow eyes regarded them unblinkingly.


Sinde awoke suddenly, shivering violently, her heart

pumping in her breast. She lay staring up into the blackness, aware of the distant pounding of the sea and the slow regular breathing of Trayim beside her.

Something had awoken her; something had nudged her subconscious into wakefulness.

The sorceress caught and held her breath and then slipped into a slow regular rhythm. One by one her senses shut down; sight first, although she did not notice it in the blackness of the cave, then hearing – the whisper of the sea and Trayim's breathing faded and were replaced by a low ceaseless hum. Touch went next – the warm feather touch of her companion's skin, the roughness of the blanket and the stone floor beneath ... and then she was floating in a featureless grey void. She waited a moment and then sank deeper into herself – and a semblance of sight returned. Pastel hues formed and quickly deepened into vivid colours; Trayim's sleeping body was outlined in an aura of brilliant crimson, whilst the cave growths glowed amber and warm bronze.

Sinde willed herself forward and outside the cave. The cloudy black night came alive with colour and light. She could distinguish the auras of the remainder of the group, the brighter and starker auras of those that were awake and alert, and in the next cave, the blinding aura of a couple in the throes of passion.

She floated higher and began to tone out the usual auras, and gradually the night drifted back into shade. The sorceress expanded her perception, and then she felt the first malevolent tendrils of an alien presence. Her shields flared as she caught sight of the bone-white light and then she was falling ... falling ... falling. She stopped above the harsh pulsating glow and allowed the night to come alive again with colour and light. She attempted to make sense of the colours below her: a blood-red aura tinged with black and surrounding a hard knot of cold white light. It was human – but only vaguely so; smaller, broader, the arms unnaturally long, the head abnormally large. She probed, attempting to read any signs of intelligence – but there was nothing, only a cold terrible hatred and a ravenous hunger.

The creature moved, and Sinde was suddenly aware that it was creeping towards a bright human aura. She fled back to her own body, the night dissolving into flame around her and then bursting into pain as circulation abruptly returned to her numb limbs. She cried out – and then Trayim was beside her, her small hands cradling her head.

'Outside ... outside ...' she gasped, 'alarm ...'

Trayim pulled the dagger from beneath her pillow and darted out into the night. 'Leos, Inde,' she called. She heard the scuff of bare feet on stone as the two guards came running. 'There is something out here,' she said urgently, 'waken the others.'

Leos, one of Ain's hunters, nodded, only her eyes and teeth visible in the darkness, and slipped off towards the other caves. Inde, one of Trayim's countrywomen, stayed by her side, a long shaft of fire-hardened wood held across her body.

A pebble rattled off the stones and Trayim spun around, her knife hand coming up, her eyes probing the darkness. She sensed something moving and then she caught a rank beast odour. She opened her mouth to cry out and then the creature was upon her. The knife was struck from her hand and went spinning down amongst the rocks. Inde screamed and struck down with her spear, but the shaft snapped against a stone, and then she suddenly realised that she dare not strike again for fear of hitting her mistress.

Trayim struggled beneath the beast's weight, its foul fur against her mouth and in her eyes. She felt its short blunt fingers tearing at her flesh, and its snapping fangs were dangerously near her throat. She drove her straightened fingertips into the creature's side, and at the same time drove her knee upwards into its groin. The beast grunted and then howled as the knee rammed home. It shifted its

13

grip on her arms and its wide hands found her throat; its fingers locked and it began to squeeze.

Trayim gasped and choked, struggling for breath. Her lungs laboured and her head began to pound. Tiny spots of colour danced before her eyes and there was a roaring in her ears. Her feebly waving arms attempted to break the beast's hold, to plunge her fingers into its eyes, but it kept snapping at her, its teeth clicking alongside the palm of her hand. The spots of colour before her eyes intensified . . . And then the sky exploded with light.

Trayim had a momentary glimpse of a broad sloping brow and tiny eyes and then it was gone. Hands grabbed her and dragged her away, scraping her already torn flesh on the rough sand and stone, but she pushed them away and sat up.

Overhead the night sky was aflame with a brilliant red globe that hovered just above head height, crackling and spitting. In the crimson light she could see the huge figure of Cipine outlined against the darkness, the muscles in her arms and torso rippling as she held the squirming beast high above her head, laughing as she evaded the flailing paws.

A shadow moved out of the night and Ain the Huntress joined the northerner. She gazed up at the creature for a moment and then slipped her green stone knife from its sheath along her forearm. The huntress stood back and nodded to Cipine. The mercenary grinned and threw the creature at Ain's feet; she stooped, the blood-lust running liquid through her ebony body, and the stone knife glittered before it came away dripping.

Abruptly the globe of fire sputtered and shrank in upon itself and for a moment the witch-light danced around Sinde before it disappeared.

In the silence that followed the pounding of the waves seemed unnaturally loud, and the hiss of the surf on the shore seemed almost menacing, but then someone called for torches and the shouts broke the spell.

14

Caesir appeared in the cave mouth with Fintane, and hurried down the beach, a naked short-sword in her hand. She glanced back at her betrothed, and snarled in disgust as she noted that he held back, making sure that the danger was past. By the time she reached the beast's carcass Sinde was kneeling beside Trayim, her delicate hands running down her lover's body, checking for broken bones or cracked ribs. The Mistress of Craftswomen was badly bruised, scratched and torn, but none of her wounds was serious. The sorceress helped her to her feet and half carried her up to their cave where she had a small supply of salves and ointments which would help heal the wounds.

Caesir joined Cipine and Ain standing over the body of the creature. She nudged it with the flat of her sword, but it didn't move: its throat had been expertly cut from ear to ear.

'What is it?' she asked flatly.

'Beast-man,' Cipine said without hesitation. 'In the forests of my homeland they are sometimes found in small colonies. Perhaps they were once men that had lived wild and degenerated into beasts,' she suggested.

Ain knelt and, in the light of the flickering torches, turned the creature over. She shook her head. 'No, I've seen this type before in my homeland,' she said slowly. She glanced up at the princess. 'Surely you recognise the beast?'

Caesir frowned. 'It is not unfamiliar; but this is less brutish than the animals I once saw in the floating menagerie.'

The huntress prised open the protruding jaws and examined the broad teeth. 'There are two types,' she said in her deep, mellow voice, 'the man-beast and the beast-man. The first is a creature that although outwardly manlike is a wild beast, both shy and gentle; the second is not a beast, but not yet a man – it is something caught in between.' She looked up at Caesir and Cipine. 'This is a beast-man, and look at these teeth ... it is a meat eater,' she added quietly.

Cipine laughed humourlessly. 'We must have seemed like

a gift from the gods to this creature.'

Caesir nodded. 'A gift indeed – and I dare say it was not alone. They will be back.' She glanced up at the sky which was already lightening in the east. 'The night is almost done. Call in your sentries Cipine, double the guards around the caves and keep the fires burning.' She looked over at Ain. 'Will they be back tonight?'

'I doubt it, not tonight – but tomorrow perhaps, or the day after, but they will be back.'

The princess tapped the palm of her hand with the flat of her sword. 'Well, there is little we can do for the remainder of this night, but in the morning...' She looked at both Ain and Cipine.

The huntress nodded. 'We'll scout this creature's trail back to its lair...'

'And then what?' the mercenary asked, a grin already beginning to spread across her face.

Ain laughed. 'And then you'll get a chance to quench that battle-thirst you have.'

Caesir made her way up the beach to the sorceress' cave. She found Trayim sleeping peacefully on a thick blanket with Sinde kneeling over her, gently rubbing a malodorous salve onto her naked body. She looked up as the princess entered.

'Is it dead?' And then she nodded and answered her own question. 'Yes, it is dead.' She turned her attention back to her companion and resumed smearing the salve over a dark ugly bruise beneath Trayim's left breast.

'How bad is she?'

Sinde shook her head. 'Not bad. Bruised, cut, a cracked rib. She was lucky...' The sorceress moved aside and allowed Caesir to see the dark, regularly spaced bruisemarks around Trayim's throat.

The princess nodded. 'She was lucky,' she said softly. 'She saved our lives... but it was you who gave the warning?'

16

Sinde nodded. 'I felt it; it was cold, so cold, filled with nothing but the desire to kill... and kill... and kill... and feed!' She shuddered.

'We will destroy them,' Caesir promised.

The sorceress turned her head and the flickering torchlight touched her red-rimmed eyes. 'If you do not then they will surely destroy us all.'

The princess nodded silently. She stood in the mouth of the cave for a few moments watching the sorceress work and then turned back into the night.

Sinde meticulously covered Trayim's entire body with the healing salve and then, with herb-scented water, washed her hands. She then slipped off her robe and lay down beside her companion. Trayim moved in her sleep and her arm snaked across Sinde's shoulders. The sorceress adjusted the thick blanket over them both and then held her tight.

'...And so,' Caesir concluded, 'if we are to survive in this strange land, we must bear children.' She paused and looked at each one of the faces of the women gathered below the mouth of the cave. Many of them had been taken as slaves to her father's palace, torn from their tribes and nations. Some had been born slaves and others, like Cipine's viragos, were escaped slaves and runaway freewomen. This island had represented a chance for them to experience true freedom... but now they were being forced to submit themselves to a man.

'We will divide into three groups; one group to each man: Fintane, Bith and Landra.' She hurried on, aware of the growing murmur of indignation. 'The three groups will then settle in different parts of the island...'

'And do what?' one of the women demanded savagely.

Caesir leaned forward, her eyes and voice chill. 'We will survive!' She allowed her gaze to roam over the group again. 'There is no choice in this matter – anyone who does not consent will be slain out of hand.' Her voice hardened. 'Is that understood?'

And this time there was no reply.


Ain carefully parted the long grass and peered down into the small valley that bordered the sheltered beach.

Cipine, lying on the hard ground beside her, swore quietly.

'By the gods, I didn't realise there were so many.'

Ain's dark eyes probed the hillside, seeking signs of habitation. She stiffened and nudged the mercenary in the ribs; Cipine edged forward and grunted. Almost directly below them the hillside was riddled with caves and the slopes below them were rank with excrement and the remains of birds and small animals. Lower down the slopes were the beast-men – scores of them. At first glance Cipine reckoned that there must be close on three times their own number – and that wasn't counting the females or young, who could probably be counted on to fight in any case.

'We'll never take them,' she said quietly.

'Look,' Ain said suddenly, moving back and allowing the mercenary to slide across to her position. Cipine followed her arm. 'There is only one entrance,' Ain said slowly, 'only one way in...'

'...Only one way out.' Cipine stared at the cleft, a ragged knife-slit in the mountainside, barely wide enough for two to stand abreast. She looked across at the huntress. 'If we can hold the cleft...'

Ain nodded. 'The beast-men are meat eaters, but do you see any game down there?'

'Nothing.'

'Then they must hunt abroad for it. And if we can take and hold that entrance, we can contain the creatures within the valley... hunger will soon turn them upon themselves.'

'What about the trees, the bushes?' Cipine argued.

18

'Burn them. And the fire should terrorise the beast-men.'

The mercenary nodded slowly. 'It could be done ... and it might just work. But instead of trying to hold the entrance, why not just block it with a landslide, and post guards up along here to discourage any climbers.'

'Yes! Although the cliff-face may be just a little too steep even for them.'

'And what about the sea?'

'The beast-men fear the water, they will not venture out into the waves.'

Cipine nodded again. 'It might just work.'


In the light of a tiny fire just inside the mouth of a cave Ain and Cipine carefully outlined their plan to Caesir, Sinde and Trayim. The princess listened intently, elbows resting on her knees, her chin cupped in her palms. When they were finished she sat back against the rough cold wall and knuckled her tired eyes. 'Is there no other way?' she asked at last. 'Must we begin our rule of this land with slaughter ... or would it be genocide?' She turned to Sinde. 'You said that they have the capability to become true men in time?'

The sorceress nodded. 'In time, yes. But we will not see it, nor our children, nor our children's children.'

'They are animals,' Ain gently reminded her, 'intelligent, dangerous animals, and like all animals they are governed by instincts ... but they are not human!'

'Is there no other way to kill them then; something swifter, less lingering...?'

'What's got into you, girl?' Cipine snapped, 'you've never had scruples before. I've seen you order a slave slain for dropping your comb; I've watched you wager on the man-fights; I've hunted the devil-fish with you and watched you kill without compunction or pity ... and now you're cribbing over the death of a pack of wild animals.'

'This afternoon,' Caesir said quietly, staring deep into the

19

fire, 'I divided the women up amongst the three men. I did it by lot but, as I've already said, you Ain will go with Landra, you Cipine with my father ...' She raised a slim elegant hand as the mercenary opened her mouth to protest. 'I know your tastes do not run to men – but there is nothing else to be done; besides, he is an old man with fifteen other women to contend with, and you may be just a little too big and a little too mean for him.'

The mercenary nodded glumly.

'But first we must take care of the beasts,' the princess continued. 'Your plan is sound, and if there is no other way, then put it into effect as quickly as possible. And that valley sounds very enticing,' she added.

Ain nodded. 'It's good land, but it's been hunted out. The bay however is sheltered, the fishing would be good.'

'Excellent. When the beasts are gone we can settle one of the groups in it. Will the beast-men come tonight?' she then asked Sinde, changing the subject.

The sorceress shook her head. 'I don't know. I can only sense their rage and hunger once they near me.'

Ain nudged the fire with her calloused foot, sending sparks spiralling upwards against the ceiling. 'It's possible – no, probable, but this,' she nodded at the fire, 'is our greatest protection. If we build a vast fire in the cave mouths and then double the guards we should be safe.'

Cipine stood. 'I'll set a few traps with stones, sticks and some jars; at least they'll give us some warning when the beasts come.'


The beast-men came that night. Caesir, lying near the back of the largest cave in Fintane's arms, heard the sudden clatter of stones and then a jar breaking, and knew immediately that something prowled outside the cave, skulking in the darkness beyond the fires. She shook Fintane, but he only moaned and rolled over. The princess spat in disgust; in the past few moons she had learned much about her betrothed. She slipped from beneath the furs and, pulling one across her naked shoulders, padded on bare feet down to the mouth of the cave and the leaping flames. She found both Cipine and Ain already there, fully armed and in their leather kirtles, breastplates and helms. Sinde and Trayim, who had moved from their own smaller cave, joined them a moment later.

Caesir turned to the sorceress. 'How many?'

'Many. A score, perhaps more. They can smell us; we are fresh meat.' She smiled. 'In these confined caves our odours must be appetising.'

Cipine growled like a wild bear. 'The first one to stick its head in here will feed on my sword,' she swore.

'If it doesn't run from your ugly face first,' Ain added.

'Well, you're all right – it won't even see you,' Cipine retorted, 'unless you open your eyes or smile at it ... and then you'll more than likely blind it.'

Landra joined them, a curved sickle in one hand and a long flat-bladed knife in the other. The pilot was as tall as Ain and blacker, but his eyes had a yellowish tinge and his teeth were stained and blackened. 'Are they there?' he asked slowly, his accent thickening his words.

A stone rattled down the beach and then another jar shattered, answering him.

Something moved in the night beyond the fire and flat yellow eyes glinted briefly in the light and then something sailed in through the flames and bounced off the walls. The small group fell back as more stones rattled off the walls and ceiling.

Ain knelt and gathered up a few of the large round stones. She waited until she caught a glimpse of movement and then flung a stone out through the flames. A howl of pain testified to the accuracy of her aim. A spate of missiles clattered about the cave, and was then followed by silence. Ain tossed a few more stones out into the darkness, but they only rattled harmlessly down the beach. Cipine edged closer to the mouth of the cave, her broad double-edged sword naked in her hand. She squeezed her eyes almost shut against the fire's glare and squinted out into the night. Something moved at the corner of her eye and she turned – just as the first of the beast-men came flying in over the flames. She reacted unthinkingly, throwing herself forward and down, bringing her sword up: disembowelling the creature. It thrashed about in a pool of its own blood and innards until the huge mercenary stooped and, catching it at groin and neck, hoisted it up over her head and tossed it out over the flames back onto the beach. The savage screams which had risen during the sudden attack died again, and silence once more fell on the beach – to be replaced by a hideous snarling, such as dogs make over a bone.

The remainder of the night passed quietly. A few stones were thrown into the cave, but nothing else attempted to brave the fire. As the sky paled towards dawn the small group broke up, leaving Cipine and Landra standing by the greying ashes. The ebony pilot stood in the mouth of the cave, staring out wistfully at the sea breaking on the rough beach.

Cipine glanced across at him. 'Why don't you come back from there,' she growled, 'they may still be out there.'

Landra shook his head. 'They are creatures of the night,' he replied, 'they've already returned to their lairs.'

'How do you know?'

'We have them in my homeland,' he said turning around to face her. 'They are not true animals; in my country the wise men say that they are the spirits of men condemned to walk this world for their crimes.'

Cipine laughed at the belief. 'My gods may be harsh but they are fair.'

'You are of the north,' the pilot said, a statement rather than a question, 'a mercenary, pirate and worse,' – Cipine grinned broadly – 'leader of a band of wild warrior women...' he paused and added softly, 'and you have been given to me.'

The mercenary went suddenly chill. 'I have been given to no one. I understood that I had been allotted to the old man to try and bear at least one child, and since I would not ask my troops to do anything that I myself would not try, I will do that. Where do you come in?' she demanded loudly.

Landra grinned broadly. 'I won you in a fair wager – and I rather think the old man was pleased to lose you.'

Cipine's knuckles whitened about the pommel of her sword. 'Well, I am honour bound to accept that,' she said coldly, 'but,' she added warningly, 'do not expect me to take any pleasure from the act, and I've heard also that you find inflicting pain to your liking. Try that with me – and I'll break you in two!' Cipine turned on her heel and walked away, leaving Landra staring after her, a curious smile playing about his thick lips.


Trayim's delicate long-fingered hands touched the huge slab of stone. 'It is weak here... and here,' she said softly. 'Strike it – *hard* – and the whole wall will come down.'

Cipine ran her hard calloused hand down the seemingly smooth surface of the rock face. 'How do you know?'

The easterner smiled shyly. 'I am a craftswoman; I have worked with many materials, including stones, semi-precious and otherwise. This rock is flawed, take my word for it.'

The mercenary grunted and then glanced over her broad shoulder at Ain. 'What do you think?'

Ain looked up at the sheer walls of the ravine rising on either side. The narrow band of sky high above them was startlingly blue against the blackness of the stone. 'If Trayim says it will come down...' she said doubtfully.

'And how are you going to knock it down?' Cipine asked.

Trayim smiled and shook her head. 'I'm not – you are!'

23

'Me?'

'You,' the craftswoman insisted, 'you alone have the strength.' She pointed at the stone. 'You will strike the rock here!'

'And then?' the mercenary demanded.

'You run.'

One of Cipine's warriors came back down the ravine towards them. She stopped and bowed briefly. 'The creatures are sleeping; most of them down by the shore, but a few on the slopes. However there is nothing moving up this end.'

Trayim looked at Cipine and Ain. 'Is all in readiness?'

'My warriors are in position along the cliff tops,' Cipine said. 'As soon as this wall comes down those beast-men are going to try scrambling up – and we'll be waiting for them.'

'We'll then send a few fire-arrows in,' Ain added, 'just to help things along.'

Trayim nodded and turned away, followed by Ain and the warrior, and slipped quickly down the ravine into the shadows. Cipine walked slowly down the defile towards the opening that led out into the enclosed valley. She stood concealed in the shadows and stared down towards the golden beach. The sun was slanting in across the mountains, dappling the greenery, reminding her of the great forests of her homeland, and the small picket-enclosed village amidst the thick dark trunks that was the abiding memory of her youth. Angrily she shook the memory aside.

The beast-men were lying across the lush grass in small groups of three or four. Some tossed and turned restlessly in the warm afternoon heat, whilst others moved listlessly along the shore, but keeping well clear of the sparkling waves. She made a rough count; Ain's scouts had reported that all the beast-men had returned from their night's hunting – but even if only one escaped, it might endanger their own small foothold on the tiny isle. They had to kill them all in one go. It wasn't a clean death – but the women were outnumbered.

The huge mercenary returned to the stone Trayim had marked. She found Mila, one of her guards, already there, holding Cipine's huge mace in both hands. Cipine nodded her thanks and, instructing her to wait, began to unbuckle her heavy armour. She stripped off everything: greaves, breastplate, helmet, knife and sword. Mila bundled the weapons and armour in her arms and staggered down the ravine, leaving Cipine alone, clad only in a light shift and sandals before the marked stone.

She spat into her cupped palms, bent over and lifted the mace easily, although Mila had had to struggle to carry it to her. It was a huge stone ball with a natural hole running directly through the centre. Into the hole Cipine had fitted a short handle: a highly polished branch from an ancient oak tree wound around with strips of seasoned leather. Leather bands also encircled the ball, and these had been fitted with shards of metal. The northerner could swing the mace one-handed – and the results were devastating.

She now stood directly in front of the marked stone, her broad feet set firmly into the soft ground, her columnar thighs tensed. She slipped her right hand into the leather thong and began to swing the mace gently to and fro. Her left hand gripped the haft just above her right and her knuckles began to whiten. Her breathing deepened and regulated as it always did before a battle, and she could feel the pulse pounding at her throat, temples and breast.

And then she swung at the stone.

The mace struck the spot Trayim had marked – and shattered. Both of Cipine's arms went numb and she could feel every bone in her body shake with the blow. Chips of the shattered ball flew back and stung her face and neck like angry insects. She staggered backwards, turned and started to run – and fell. For a moment she lay there, trembling ...

and then she suddenly realised that it wasn't her trembling – it was the entire ravine. The mercenary heaved herself to her feet; her arms were still numb and tingling, her wrists and shoulders ached, and even her ribs hurt, and she wondered whether she had cracked some with the force of her blow. She glanced back over her shoulder: there was a visible dent in the stone where she had struck it and radiating out from the depression was a series of ever widening cracks. Even as she watched they raced up the slab and large chips of stone dropped down. The air was suddenly filled with whirling dust motes which stung the eyes and caught at the throat. Cipine threw herself forward and rolled to one side as a flurry of rocks and large stones tumbled down from the heights just behind her. She pushed herself to her feet and raced for the end of the ravine, dodging the larger stones that were falling now. And then there was a loud crack as the entire side of the cliff-face fell inwards behind her. The concussion threw her forward again and she covered her head with her hands as jagged lumps of stone hurtled past. A score or more bit deeply into her back and thighs, and a larger piece struck her a glancing blow just above the ear that left her dazed and sickened. She grew aware of voices, and then hands gripping her under the arms, dragging her to her feet, supporting her down the length of the defile, while the walls collapsed in behind them. She looked up and glimpsed a long bar of light, and then the whirling dust blotted it out, and then there was nothing.

Two white staring eyes in a black-skinned face swam into view; she blinked and they divided into two. Cipine blinked again and Ain and Landra's faces separated and solidified. The mercenary attempted to sit up, but Ain pushed her firmly down.

'What happened?' she whispered eventually, surprised at how weak her voice sounded.

'The rock face fell in,' Ain said, 'just as Trayim said it

would. Unfortunately, you were struck several times by falling rocks.'

'And the ravine?' Cipine croaked, her throat raw with dust.

'Is blocked,' Landra supplied. He was kneeling by her side, looking intently at her ... and Cipine suddenly realised that she was naked, the ragged and bloody remains of her shift lying balled at her feet. For some reason his smile disturbed her and she felt a sudden surge of anger. She glared up at him. He saw her look and smiled insolently and allowed his gaze to drift slowly down her body, lingering briefly on her huge breasts before drifting lower.

Cipine pushed herself into a sitting position, closing her eyes as the world swam around her and pulsed blackly in time to her pounding head. When she opened her eyes, Landra was gone and Caesir now knelt beside her. The princess smiled and nodded. 'It is done. The beast-men are trapped; some have attempted to scale the cliff-face, but your warriors have forced them back.' The princess leaned forward, gave Cipine her hand and helped her to her feet. 'We have a lot to thank you for.'

The mercenary shrugged, and then winced as her head renewed its pounding. 'I'm not pleased with what I've done,' she said quietly, 'it will be a terrible death for them.'

Caesir nodded. 'I know; that is how I feel, but it is necessary; there was no choice – as you yourself pointed out.'

'And now?'

Caesir smiled. 'We wait; time and hunger will do our work for us.'


Landra came for Cipine that night. The mercenary awoke with the sound of ragged breathing above her. Her nostrils dilated as she caught the rank animal odour of stale sweat on the heavy atmosphere, and she immediately knew who was standing there. Her hand closed about the dagger beneath

27

the rolled cloak that doubled as a pillow.

A foot nudged her side. 'Wake up.'

She lay unmoving for a moment and then slowly rolled over on her side with a groan. 'What... what is it?'

There was a rustle by her side and then a sweat-slick hand brushed her thigh. 'It's me,' the pilot said hoarsely.

Cipine sat up slowly, still feigning drowsiness. 'What do you want?' she mumbled.

The warm damp hand moved slowly upwards. 'I have come for you; we will lie together this night.' The pilot's breath was raw and foul against her face. He moved closer and then lay down beside her, and Cipine, who had fought her way from one end of a barbaric continent to the other, braving unimaginable horrors and terrors, shrank from the southerner's touch. Landra laughed. 'Why so shy, surely you do not fear me?'

'I fear no man,' Cipine said coldly.

'Well then, I think it's time you learned!' The pilot gripped her flesh and twisted, while his other hand found her shoulder and pushed her back to the cold stone. He lowered his body over hers and she felt his sour breath warm on her cheek. Cipine struck inwards with the edge of her hand, catching Landra just beneath the ribs, pushing him off her. He growled like an animal as he came to his feet, and Cipine heard the dry rasp of a blade being withdrawn. The mercenary smiled grimly and moved into a fighting stance: she was going to cut this bastard into fish bait.

Landra moved and Cipine dodged instinctively, turning her body to one side and stabbing inwards with her knife hand where she imagined the southerner to be. Her blade caught flesh briefly and then pulled free, and then she threw herself backwards as she felt the other change direction. In the total darkness she felt the whip of a knife blade above her head, and she knew that for that instant Landra was off balance. Cipine kicked upwards with the flat of her foot, catching him full in the groin. He screamed like an animal and fell to the ground retching. Following the sounds, Cipine kicked him again, and his teeth clicked together like two stones striking, and his head bounced off the ground.

The mercenary realised that she would have to finish it quickly now; Landra's screams had attracted attention and already she could hear shouts. She moved in until her foot touched his quivering leg. Sure of herself now, she stepped forward and then brought her foot down full force between the pilots legs. He howled like a gutted stallion and continued screaming until the mercenary drove her knife up through his jaw into the brain.

The morning was sharp and chill and the waves sweeping in from the south were grey and sombre. Caesir shivered and pulled her heavy woollen cloak tighter about her slim shoulders. She looked at Sinde walking by her side and shook her head in wonderment, for the sorceress was clad in nothing more than a thin white shift that was moulded to her tiny figure by the wind.

'Are you not cold?'

Sinde shook her head. 'I learned as a very young girl how to control and regulate my body.' She reached over and touched Caesir's hand. The princess started: the easterner's hand was warm and dry.

They continued walking in silence and then Caesir suddenly asked, 'What are we going to do now?'

'He was a brutal, violent man; all the women he lay with bore the bruises and cuts of his lust; he took pleasure in pain.'

'But Cipine didn't have to kill him!' Caesir protested.

'They were fighting in the dark,' Sinde reminded her.

The princess nodded. 'I know that. I also know that Cipine is one of the deadliest fighters either in or outside the arena. I once watched her fight three men – criminals – at the one time... and she was blindfolded. She dispatched them without even being touched.'

The sorceress shrugged. 'He was of little use in any case; of the eight or ten women he bedded – even though at least half were fertile at the time – none have conceived.' The sorceress continued gazing out across the white-capped waves, and her eyes glazed. After a moment she blinked slowly and then turned away from the sea and looked up the beach towards the caves. 'He has left us nothing but his blood.' Her voice changed, becoming distant and gentle. 'When we are gone,' she said softly, 'and our names have all but been forgotten, he will be remembered: Landra, the first dead man in the land of Caesir Banba.' She turned away and walked quickly up the beach, leaving the princess standing by the hissing waves, strangely troubled.

Later that morning Caesir climbed the cliffs to stand beside Ain and Cipine, and stare down into the valley. The slopes directly below them were covered with thick dark blood where the guards had forced back the beast-men. At the foot of the cliffs, a broken-limbed corpse was being dragged away by two of the creatures.

'What will they do with it?' Caesir asked.

'Eat it,' Ain said without turning around. 'They will feed off their own dead for a while.'

'And then?'

'Then the stronger will start killing the smaller and weaker... and then the survivors will start killing off each other.'

Caesir turned to Cipine. 'What did you do with Landra's body?'

The mercenary smiled, and continued smiling as Caesir's gaze snapped downwards and then back to the mercenary's face. She shivered and turned away, suddenly terrified. Her dream, which had grown during the long voyage, of starting afresh in this new land, was rapidly crumbling into dust.

The beast-men were vermin, lower than slaves or animals: they had to be wiped out. But now one of their own number was dead, his carcass tossed to the animals to be devoured, and no matter what he was or what he had done his corpse deserved a little more respect, and Caesir came from a race that welcomed death and the new beginning it brought and had a horror of the desecrated corpse. And for the first time the princess realised that she was no longer in control; Ain, Cipine, Tayim and Sinde held the reins of power, for while they each controlled one facet of life on this tiny island, she had nothing.

And she wondered then what would become of her ... indeed, what would become of them all?


The beast-men died surprisingly quickly, and in the end it was their own viciousness that killed them off. In the confined space of the valley tempers quickly grew short and violent, and bloody arguments ensued ... with the victor eating the tastier morsels of the loser and leaving the corpse to rot beneath the sun. The rotting corpses soon attracted swarms of black insects that had plagued the Caesirians around their fires, and then the vermin arrived.

They never did discover how the rats arrived on the island; perhaps they had been there all along, living in warrens underground. Two days after Cipine had slain Landra, the guards on the cliff tops reported that black shadows were drifting across the ground and engulfing the corpses. It was Ain with her sharp eyes who made out the countless small furry bodies.

And four days after that the plague struck.

The symptoms were terrifyingly familiar to the women who had lived along the banks of the Nile, and who had lived with the constant threat of plague. It manifested itself with swellings in the armpits and groin, followed by fever, bleeding, muscle tremors ... and death.

Even Sinde's magic couldn't combat the invisible killer, and in a matter of days it had devastated the small group. Ironically Cipine, for all her great strength and stamina, was one of the first to fall, swiftly followed by Ain and Trayim. Bith, Caesir's father, was one of the last to die, but Fintane drank a concoction of his own devising, and died swiftly and easily.

In the latter days the few women who remained gathered all the bodies together in a great pile, and for a day and a night the cleansing flames leapt and raged, reddening the night sky and darkening the day with heavy clouds. Caesir lingered a few days after the last of the women had died, struggling vainly to the end. And Sinde buried her by the seashore where, generations later, the Partholonians would discover and puzzle over the bones.'*

The sorceress walked the cliffs in the evening of that final day. Smouldering embers still glowed in the heart of the great funeral pyre, and sparks and cinders drifted across the beach and draped the low grave-mound with wreaths of fire. The eastern sorceress shivered in the evening breeze and smiled grimly, remembering her last conversation with the princess.

Caesir had been close to death, her once proud beauty gone forever, her fine features bloated and her body wasted. Speech was difficult and the sorceress had to strain to hear her.

'Is this ... retribution?'

Sinde shook her head.

'But if we had not killed the beast-men and Landra, surely the rats wouldn't have come?' she whispered brokenly.

Again Sinde shook her head. 'No, they were here all the time, they would have come out sooner or later.'

* see 'The Dawn' *Irish Folk And Fairy Tales* vol. II. chap. 1

'The blood... the blood attracted them.'

Reluctantly the sorceress nodded.

'In your homeland, does the land itself have a soul?' the princess asked, her eyes bright and glistening.

Sinde nodded. 'We call it the *anima*, the spirit of life.'

'This is a young land,' Caesir whispered sadly, 'I fear we have let it taste blood too soon; I fear it may develop a taste for it.' She shuddered. 'May the gods forgive us for what we have done.'

Sinde blinked. The wind was cold on the cliff-top. The fever had her, she knew, and soon she would drift off into that final sleep and the rats would have her bones. She looked down into the valley, but already night's shadows had claimed it, and there was nothing moving, and no sound from it save the stunted trees rustling in the breeze. She walked on. Coloured spots danced before her eyes and then she doubled up as pain lanced through her. Images – like smoke-dreams – flashed behind her eyes; curiously garbed and armoured armies marched across mist enshrouded fields ..., war chariots cut through tall waving grass ... stately processions wound along polished gleaming roads ... a golden-haired warrior lay slumped against a pillar, a raven perched on his shoulder ... white-robed priests chanted in the midst of dark forests ... long-prowed ships rode the waves ... dark-cowled monks fell beneath their axes ... gold and bronze banners flapped in the wind ... gold and bronze ... gold ... bronze ...

Sinde blinked. She found herself standing on the cold stones of the cliff-top staring out across the waves towards the west into the sunset. Gold and bronze burned across the sky. She blinked again and for a single instant it turned red like freshly spilled blood. She staggered and looked down. Far, far below her the waves pounded against the cliffs in white-foamed fury. And then the foam too was touched with frothy pink. There was blood on this land, there was death also ... its history would be a bloody one ... blood and bronze and gold ...

And blackness.

*'From the east they came, the princess, the warrior, the huntress, the craftswoman, the sorceress, and their followers. They fled the waves and found the land, and death claimed them.'*

# Chapter Two

## I – THRICE CURSED

Ebblue sat up suddenly, pushing the sleeping body off her, her head tilting to one side, listening. Beside her Necca rolled over and groaned and she immediately clamped a hand over his mouth. His dark brown eyes snapped open and he struggled for a moment to sit up. His stepmother looked down and shook her head silently, her right hand pointing towards the door. Necca's eyes registered understanding and he slipped from the bed furs and padded naked to the window ledge where he had left his knife and clothes.

There was a sudden clatter of metal off stone in the corridor outside and his knife snicked wetly as it slid from its oiled sheath. He jumped over the rumpled bed and stood with his broad back flat against the cold stones by the door, the knife in his right hand held flat against his thigh. Ebblue threw back the covers and crossed to the huge fireplace, smiling regretfully at Necca. He grinned as he watched her reach up and unhook the crossed hunting spears from above the mantel and hurry back to his side. Naked, carrying the two spears, she looked like the Morrigan – the Goddess of Death – in her human form. She pressed herself against him, her flesh warm against his, her breasts brushing his arm, and her breath on his neck. And together they waited for what they both realised would be her husband's and his father's guards.

There was a soft scratching at the door, and then a hoarse

voice whispered, 'Necca ... Necca ...'

Necca looked down at Ebblue; they both recognised the voice. It was Rian, his brother's. He raised his eyebrows in a silent question, and his stepmother nodded.

Necca eased the latch up with his free hand, and the door swung silently inwards. Rian stepped into the room – and stopped with the point of a spear pricking his throat.

'Slowly, brother, slowly,' Necca whispered, 'are you alone?'

Rian nodded, and then winced as the spear point tore his flesh. 'I'm alone, but by the Dagda and Danu, you've got to get out of here.' He pushed the spear down and swung around to face his brother and stepmother. His eyes widened momentarily at their nakedness and then he hurried on. 'Father knows! Someone – Bona I think – has told him, and he's on his way here now, with a company of guards ...'

He stopped suddenly as Ebblue raised her hand. 'Someone's coming,' she snapped.

Rian went white. 'What are you going to do?' he demanded. 'You're trapped.'

Necca smiled coldly. 'There's not a lot we can do now, is there. But you brother, you can hide ...' he gestured towards a huge ornate wooden chest.

Rian shook his head and drew his knife. 'We've grown and played together, we've learned and ...' he glanced across at his stepmother, who was not in fact much older than himself, 'loved together. Let us now die together.'

Necca smiled and, pulling his brother close, embraced him. 'What more does a man need,' he said quietly, 'than the love of a woman and the loyalty of a brother?'

Rian smiled quietly. 'Shouldn't you both ... put something on?' he suggested. 'Things are going to be bad enough as it is without you both inflaming the situation by father finding you naked and,' he glanced at the long furrows down his brother's back and the red bite marks on Ebblue's breasts, 'all the signs of a night's passion on you.'

The tall dark-haired warrior grinned. 'You were always wiser than me, little brother,' he said, 'you would have made a fine poet or a druid.'

Rian stood with his ear to the door while both Ebblue and Necca dressed hurriedly. The early morning sun, slanting in through the small high window, caught the whirling dust motes and touched them with gold and bronze. The glittering motes lingered briefly on the two lovers, uniting them in a band of sparkling light, and Rian, looking across at them, smiled bitterly. They were made for each other; they were perfectly matched, both in years and needs, and yet the quirk of fate that had brought them together would never allow them openly to proclaim their love.

Marid MacCairde, King of Munster, had married for the second time, nearly eight years after the death of his first wife. It was a surprise move, and even more surprising when he had chosen the daughter of one of the western seaboard chieftains, a small dark-haired, dark-eyed, full-bodied beauty who would, it was hoped, bear him fine sons, brothers for Necca and Rian, his sons and only children by his first wife.

However, almost from the first, Necca had found himself drawn to his stepmother, and although she had resisted his advances and attentions at first, she had gradually accepted her stepson first into her heart, and then into her bed. Rian had seen the signs early on and, on more than one occasion, spoken to his older brother about his growing involvement with their father's new bride. Necca had listened, and although he knew, deep down he knew, what he was doing was wrong, he was trapped: chained by shackles far stronger than iron.

And so Ebblue and Necca had become lovers, snatching stolen moments alone together whilst they hunted, or whenever Marid would fall into a drunken slumber early in the evening and it would be left for Rian to carry him to his

37

bed – after first ensuring that his brother and stepmother had had time to themselves. Rian wouldn't have said that he approved, but, realising that there was nothing he could do about it, endeavoured to further the affair discreetly, and without allowing any hint of it to reach his father.

But he knew it couldn't last for long.

Soon the servants had begun to talk, and on more than one occasion a startled herdsman had come across them frantically coupling in the tall lush grasslands that bordered Marid's domain, or the huntsman would remark how they would both disappear after a hare or hart when even the dogs had lost the scent.

Whispers had trickled back to the king, but he ignored them; he knew his son and he trusted his wife. But the seed of doubt had been sown.

And that suspicion had finally flowered into absolute certainty.

A wandering druid had come to the king's court; a small wild-eyed, dark-skinned man whose northern and eastern ancestry were clearly written on his broad brutish features. But he was a druid and well versed in the laws and ancient spells for controlling the forces of nature. For shelter and food through the coming winter months which he promised would be a hard one, the druid – Bona – promised to work his magic over Marid's fields, bringing out the best in beasts and crops.

The druid had quickly worked his way into the king's confidence, and soon Marid was coming to rely more and more on the small twisted man. And that night in a drunken stupor he had asked the druid if it were true that his son and wife were lovers.

Bona had smiled through his misshapen teeth and whispered in his raw hoarse voice. 'I'll wager your son has shared your wife's bed more times than you have.'

Rian had entered the dining hall just in time to see his father strike the druid to the ground and call for his guards.

38

A spear butt struck the door, swinging it open, and Marid stormed into the circular bedchamber. He stopped just inside the door, colour rising to his face at the sight of his two sons, both armed and waiting, with his wife behind them.

'So... this is how I find my bride – and my sons! Well, have you been taking turns with her, or perhaps both together...' Marid trailed off into incoherence.

Rian took a step forward. 'Father, you don't understand...' he began.

'I understand that I have found my two sons in my wife's – *their stepmother's* – bedchamber. I understand that at least one,' he looked at Necca, 'is not long awake, and I understand that my two sons are armed, and have drawn weapons on their own father.' The king stepped forward and then he suddenly struck Rian, sending him sprawling back against his brother. Necca caught him, and then swung the spear around so that the point was tilted towards his father. 'Your argument is not with Rian,' he said quietly, 'he is innocent.'

'But he knew, he *knew*,' Marid raved. 'He knew his brother was lying with his stepmother; he knew his father was being cuckolded behind his very back – he *knew*!'

Bona the druid slipped in behind the king and touched his shoulder; Marid shuddered and began to breathe quietly. The livid colour left his face and his fists unclenched. He ran a trembling hand through his wiry grey hair and took a step backwards. When he spoke again, his voice was calm and controlled. 'However, what is done, is done, and there is no escaping it. You must go – both of you – and you,' the harshness crept back into his voice as he glared at his wife, 'you have shamed my name. Take your belongings, your lovers, and anyone else who will follow you and go. I will not soil my hands with your blood.' The druid touched his shoulder again and the anger left the king's voice to be replaced by an unnatural calm. He turned to his sons. 'I curse you both,' he said evenly. 'You have taken my wife – who was more precious to me than the very waters of life, and so I curse you: let the water that sustains all life be your bane. You took my life from me and so I take it from you!' Marid MacCairde bowed stiffly, pushed past the druid and the warriors crowding the doorway, and marched down the silent corridor.

Bona the druid lingered for a moment, his flat, fishlike eyes regarding the trio with malicious amusement, and then his gnarled hand rose and sketched a sign in the air which went abruptly chill, and then he too turned and glided silently down the corridor.

Ebblue, Necca and Rian rode away the following morning with close on a thousand of their followers. The early morning sun cast long shadows along the ground and Rian, glancing back at the fort, saw the double shadow of his father and the druid snaking across the dew-damp grass, and for a single instant both shadows mingled and took on the shape of a huge crow – a portent of death.

And then the small druid raised his arms and the air above the fort began to crackle with suppressed forces as he wove his curse about the brothers and their followers. Dark clouds swept in from the west and rapidly obscured the heavens, blotting out the sun. Thunder rumbled and a quick spasm of lightning rippled through the clouds, illuminating them from within, and then there was silence in which the wind dropped and it seemed as if the morning held its breath – waiting. The air was heavy and tart, full of the promise of rain – which never materialised.

And then the druid began to chant, using a tongue that had been old when man first climbed down from the trees, a language that was inhuman and never meant to be shaped by human throats, and Ebblue, Necca and Rian felt the chill hand of death caress them all.

The incantation completed, the druid leaned forward and pointed one long, sticklike arm at the company. 'The water which does not come now will one day find you,' he screamed, his voice thin and high on the heavy air.

Necca laughed. 'Eat your words, old man,' he called, plucking a tiny ornate dagger from his belt and throwing it with all his might at the druid. The distance was almost a hundred paces and no one, least of all Necca himself, expected it to come even close to the druid – it was merely an act of defiance. But Ebblue leaned forward across her mount and called upon Danu to avenge her, and then she gestured, a tiny movement of the fingers, and suddenly a chill wind swept across the plain, catching the tiny glittering point, carrying it up and up . . . A stray sunbeam touched the metal, making it blaze molten in the gloom, and then it fell . . .

Bona screamed and his hands touched his throat and came away red, and then he slowly toppled from the walls and fell, like a broken limbed doll, to the hard ground beneath.

Necca, looking pale and shaken, turned back to his brother and lover. 'It seems as if the gods themselves are on our side this day.'

But Rian, having watching Ebblue while she was calling upon the goddess, could only smile uncertainly and nod.

The brothers travelled northwards, spending the first night by the shores of a small lake. The moon was high when Necca and Rian walked the perimeter of their camp, moving quietly through the massed hide and cloth tents, checking on the guards, the horses and the warriors concealed in the trees and bushes against sudden attack. They climbed a small knoll and stood on its tip, and stared down into the little valley, the moonlight washing the lake with silver and shadow to one side, and the tiny spots of fire, crimson and gold in the night on the other. Wind rustled through the trees, stirring the nearly leafless branches, whispering through the piled leaves about the trunks and roots, and the long grass hissed like water-splashed fire.

'What will become of us?' Rian asked suddenly, unconsciously keeping his voice low, loath to break the night-woven spell.

Cloth rustled and Rian guessed his brother had shrugged. 'We'll go on, find ourselves a valley with fresh water and settle down. There are enough of us to make it work.'

'Will our father come after us?' Rian wondered.

'I doubt it. Most of the people down there have friends or family back at court. He won't come after us,' he repeated softly, 'not after what happened to his pet druid.' He laughed.

'You don't think you caused that, do you?' his younger brother asked.

Necca's eyes shone whitely in the paleness of his face, and he shook his head. 'Oh, I doubt it; coincidence ... or maybe the gods *are* on our side.'

Rian turned and stared up into his brother's face. In the gloom he could barely make out the features, just an indistinct pale oval and the harsh glitter of his eyes as they roved across the small encampment. 'Necca,' he said quietly, 'you were watching your knife or the druid, I'm not sure which, but I was watching Ebblue when you made that throw. She was staring at the clouds and talking, whispering, chanting, I don't know,' he shook his head. 'But her lips were moving, and when you threw the knife, she leaned forward across the horse and spoke aloud, and I heard the name *Danu*, and then the fingers of her right hand gestured...'

'What are you trying to say?' Necca asked coldly.

'I'm not trying to say anything,' Rian said quickly, 'I'm telling you what I saw – you can draw your own conclusions.'

'And what are your conclusions?'

'I think ... I think Ebblue may have some of the Power.'

He stepped back and continued quickly. 'It is the only conclusion I can come to – and before you do or say anything hasty, why don't you ask her?'

For a long time Necca stood rigid, staring down into the encampment, and then he turned away and began to run down the incline into the camp. Rian sighed and followed him.

The tent was set a little way back from the others, in the midst of a tiny copse of trees. Hides had been stretched from tree to tree, enclosing a rough square, and on a framework of more branches and poles, waterproof hides had been thrown. The guard stationed outside the tent, tending the smoking fire, came to his feet with spear levelled as the brothers crashed out of the shadows into the clearing. He opened his mouth to call out a challenge, when he recognised first Necca and then Rian. He grounded his spear and saluted as they both passed him without a word and entered the tent. In the shifting glow from the small fire, the sentry's eyebrows rose and a smile touched his lips. So, it was true about the two of them sharing her... and at the same time too...

Within the tent all was in darkness, although the bitter stench of resin still lingered on the air where a torch had been lately extinguished. Necca stopped so suddenly that his brother stumbled into him. 'Get us some light,' he commanded. Rian grunted and, turning back, pushed through the leather flap. Without a word he pulled a burning branch from the fire, waved it through the air to bring it to a blaze and carried it back into the tent.

Inside, he found Necca standing over Ebblue who was lying bundled up in the sleeping furs. In the flickering torchlight, with the furs bundled up to her chin, and her raven hair loose and unbound, she looked curiously childlike and innocent. Necca knelt and kissed her on the forehead and her eyes snapped open: old, worldly eyes, and the illusion of innocence was shattered. She sat up and the furs

43

slipped away, revealing her full breasts, forever wiping away any lingering thoughts Rian might have had that she was childlike in any way.

'What is it? What's wrong?'

'Nothing... nothing,' Necca soothed her. He glanced across at Rian. 'My brother has something he wishes to discuss with you... with us.'

'Now? But... what time is it?' Ebblue demanded.

'The moon has reached its zenith and is beginning to sink,' Rian said quietly.

Ebblue looked from Rian to Necca. 'Can this not wait?' she asked quietly.

'I'm afraid not.' Rian put the torch to the tiny brazier and blew the kindling alight. It spat and sparked, sending tiny points of light wheeling upwards to die against the thick hide. He then ground the torch out against the earth and tossed it into a corner. 'Tell me,' he said quietly, 'what did you do when Necca threw his knife at the druid today?' The red firelight danced across his face, lending his eyes a maturity and depth they lacked in the full light of day, and for one moment Necca could see his father in him.

'What did you do?' he demanded.

'Do? I prayed,' Ebblue said softly. 'I prayed that Danu might hear my prayers for revenge.'

'If you were praying for revenge, then surely you should have prayed to the Morrigan?' Rian snapped. 'And tell me, what were your fingers doing when you were praying to the goddess, and before that, what were you doing looking into the heavens and muttering?'

'I... I...' She turned to Necca. 'What is this? What is he trying to say?'

Necca shook his head. 'I don't know – but answer him, tell him what you were doing.'

There was silence then in the tent for a long time, the trio frozen in a tableau of their own thoughts, with the same emotions: fear, anger, concern, flickering across all three faces, but for different reasons. At last Ebblue sighed and, suddenly realising that her breasts were bare, pulled the bed furs up to her chin, drew her knees up and encircled them with her arms, and then rested her chin on her covered knees. 'I have the Power,' she admitted tightly, 'but I have never used it for anything but good.' She looked up at Rian. 'When you saw me looking up into the clouds, I was trying to draw down the rain, to break the druid's spell, but he was the stronger and beat me in that. However, the effort left him exhausted and it was a simple matter to call up the wind and carry the knife to his throat. He could have brushed it aside with a similar wind, but to have done so would have meant that he would have had to relinquish control of the pent up storm, and his spell would have come to naught. He was caught in a single moment of indecision – a final moment of indecision.' She smiled and the shadows danced across her face, wiping away the harshness that had touched it while she talked. But then the smile slowly faded and the hard look came back into her eyes. 'But the spell, the curse, still remains. I'm doing the best I can to hold it in check – but sooner or later it will strike.'

'What curse?' Rian demanded.

'The curse of water – your father and the druid both cursed you to die by water.'

'When will it strike?' Necca asked slowly.

Ebblue shrugged. 'I have no way of knowing. Today, tomorrow, a season's time, a generation...'

'Can you not use your power to divine the future?' Rian asked.

Ebblue smiled. 'My power in that direction is very limited.'

'But you could tell us something?' Rian persisted.

'A little.'

Rian turned to his brother. 'Surely that is better than nothing?'

Necca stood. 'Perhaps. But do we want to know a fraction

45

of the future?' he wondered aloud. 'Is the anxiety of knowing better than the fear of not knowing?' He looked down at Ebblue. 'Read it for us then,' he said at last.

Ebblue nodded and, pushing down the furs, slipped from the bed. The warm firelight gilded her smooth skin, tanning it a light bronze. She pulled one of the furs off the bed and draped it across her shoulders before sitting down crosslegged on the cold ground. She looked up at Rian. 'Bring me a piece of coal and a knife,' she said.

When he brought the coal and handed her his knife, Ebblue drew a circle on the ground with the coal and then, taking both Necca's and Rian's hands, nicked their forefingers with the knife. The blood spattered onto the ground inside the circle and immediately darkened. Then, with the knife again, she divided the circle into four quarters, ensuring that there was one drop of blood in each quarter. Reverently she placed the knife to one side, the tip of the blade just touching the edge of the circle and pointing northwards. And then, placing both hands on her knees she closed her eyes and leaned back, her head tilted up towards the heavens, brow furrowed, and slowly, slowly, she began to call upon her Power.

Her hands clenched into fists and then the fingers splayed. Slowly they began to move up her thighs and in towards her groin where they lingered briefly before continuing on up across her flat stomach and then over her breasts where they crossed, her right hand going over her left shoulder, and her left hand to her right shoulder. She was breathing heavily now, her breasts rising and falling rapidly, the muscles in her stomach rippling and her knees trembling. She began to pant loudly and then her breath came in ragged gasps which quickly turned into groans that ended in a short shrill scream. Her head slumped forward and her hair tumbled into her lap.

Necca made a move to go to her, but Rian touched his shoulder and shook his head, and when they both looked back they found she was staring coldly at them, her eyes black and glittering like lumps of coal. They looked *old*, ancient beyond reckoning; it was as if she had touched some primal core deep within herself, dragging it to the surface. But even as they looked her expression changed, her eyes softened, the tense muscles in her head and neck relaxed and she assumed her more normal expression. A shadow of a smile touched her face, which now looked tired and worn.

'I'm sorry,' Necca said quickly, 'I didn't realise it would be so difficult for you.'

Ebblue shook her head. 'It was not that difficult... no, that's not quite true,' she quickly corrected herself. 'In a way it gets easier every time, but the reaction gets proportionally worse. However,' she shook her head, 'I reached the state of meditation necessary to draw upon the future memories...'

'*Future memories?*' Rian asked.

'Much as we remember the past, so too do we know – *remember* – the future, if only we know how to look and where to look.'

'Did you see our future?' Necca asked.

'Not one – there is never one immutable future, there are always a few, but some of course have a greater probability than others. In your – *our* – case there are many, many futures... but all with the one outcome,' she added in a whisper.

'And that is?' Rian asked, although he knew what her answer would be.

'They all end in death,' Ebblue said quietly, her voice sounding unnaturally loud in the silence.

Rian shivered suddenly in the cold night air. He had a feeling he had just been given his own death sentence, a feeling that, no matter what he did or where he went, there was no escape... a feeling of absolute hopelessness.

'And is that all?' Necca asked, 'death – just death? Is there nothing else you can tell us?'

'There is perhaps one thing,' Ebblue said doubtfully, 'I

saw a mountain pass, a long thin defile cut between two high cliffs, and on either side of the pass were two tall pillars of dark green stone. When we came to the pass we divided into two groups – one group going around the mountain, and the other through the pass. And then I felt a great disturbance, the sudden shock of mass death cut across the dream plain I inhabited... One group had been wiped out... but I don't know which group... I don't know,' she screamed, and then she buried her head in her hands and wept bitterly. Necca nodded to his brother, dismissing him, and then he went and knelt by the young woman.

The brothers and their followers continued northwards. But now they were continually harried by bandits and a sudden spell of bad weather which further slowed them down. The attacks on their camps became more and more frequent and, since they were moving through mostly open countryside with little shelter, losses, particularly among the beasts, were high.

Ten days after they had ridden away from Marid MacCairde's fort they reached the Pass of the Two Pillars. Over the previous day the character of the land had changed; from lush grassy plains it had steepened into a rock-strewn wilderness that gradually inclined upwards. And then it had levelled out and led towards the mountains of the north – and the only way through the mountains was through the pass. The alternative route was an extra ten day journey through the foothills.

The brothers led their followers along the banks of a dried-up river bed, with outriders on either tall bank and ranging far ahead and to the rear. But the countryside seemed deserted with no signs of life. Just before they reached the pass they came upon two rotting skeletons slumped beneath the branches of a spreading oak tree. Time, the elements and scavengers had dealt harshly with them, and now they were little more than white sticks poking through the rank tall grass that had sprouted from the richly fertilised earth. It was a dire omen whose significance was lost on no one in the company.

The pass was guarded by two tall pillars, remnants of the architecture of the ancient Tuatha De Danann who had once walked Erin's green fields. The pillars were carved from a heavy dark green stone and worked with tiny glyphs and pictograms. There was some evidence that a third stone had once topped the two pillar stones, much in the manner of the great stone circles in the land across the water to the east, making it a kind of gateway, but the lintel stone had long since disappeared. Down one side of the left-hand pillar was a vertical line of script in *ogham*, the incised writing form of the druids. For those with the education or training to read the lines and slashes it was a warning of *'Bane and misfortune on an evil heart or unclean spirit to pass beyond the threshold...'* Time had cleansed the latter half of the message.

And it was here the brothers parted company, for they had both recognised the location in Ebblue's warning vision, and had decided that one group should go north through the pass and the other would go around the mountain... and the gods themselves could look with favour on what group they willed.

Rian and his followers turned west and followed the foothills. The path was rough and broken, obviously ill-used, and quickly began to lead down into a small, almost bowl-shaped valley. Night was drawing in, with shadows racing in from the east, blotting out the last lingering light from the west, forcing them to camp in the valley. The night was cold, made all the more so by the ancient trees that crowded in on them. The tiny winking camp fires did little to lighten the gloom or dispel the chill and even the wind seemed to whisper portents just beyond the edge of intelligibility.

Around midnight Rian was awakened by shouts and cries to find that some of his company had come across an old woman living in a construction of branches and grasses beneath the trees. She was old, that Rian could tell immediately, a genuine oldness, not the artificial ageing that hunger and hard times touched many with. He looked into her eyes and started – for they were no longer human, and regarded him balefully and with all the intelligence of an animal.

'Why have you brought this woman here?' he asked quietly, his voice pluming whitely on the chill air.

'She was caught stealing water,' Doran, Rian's servant, answered quickly.

Rian pulled a torch from its holder and went to stand over the old woman. In the flickering light her face seemed even more frightening, with every muscle and nerve twitching and leaping. 'If you had asked, you would have been given water,' he said gently.

The old woman spat at his feet. 'My people have never asked for anything – we have always taken what we wanted. *You*!' she jabbed a bony finger in his direction, 'you did not ask my leave to enter here; this is my land, and you have trespassed.'

Rian smiled. 'We did not know this valley belonged to anyone ...'

'Do not humour me boy; I was old when your grandparents were but drooling babes. My people have held this land since time out of mind.'

'Then you must be of the De Danann,' Rian said with a smile. A ripple of laughter passed around the small group.

The old woman spun around. 'Oh, laugh if you will, but my mother was one of the People of the Goddess ... and I possess their powers!'

Rian turned away. 'Give her some water,' he said,

suddenly weary of her chatter. 'Send her on her way.'

'*Send her away, send her away,*' the old woman screeched. 'I am not your servant or hunting dog to be sent away. I am of the House of the Goddess; you will pay me all due respect and honour,' she demanded.

Rian spun around. 'Old woman this has been a long day. I have parted company with my brother and friends – and I'm not even sure if I'll ever see either him or them again. I'm tired – and you're irritating me!'

The old woman's laughter shrilled on the cold air. 'You will never see your brother again, Rian, son of Marid; neither you, nor your people will live to see the sun sink again!' She pulled away from the hands holding her. 'You have been cursed by water by one of the white-robed ones – it is fitting, aye, fitting! I too curse you, but I curse you in the name of a far older Power, for I curse you with the very soul of the land itself. Water you have kept from me – water shall be your bane!'

And she was gone. She dashed past and disappeared into the shadows behind Rian and fled into the night. Doran would have gone after her, but Rian stopped him. 'What's the point? A crazy old woman; what will you do with her?'

'But she cursed us ... she cursed us,' Doran stuttered, 'and she was of the Old Folk.' Fear had turned his face ashen in the torchlight.

'She *said* she was of the De Danann,' Rian reminded his servant, 'there is a difference.'

'But she still cursed us,' Doran repeated sullenly. 'We should go after her, make her lift the curse.'

'You will stay here,' Rian snapped, 'or I will curse you – and with more than words. Return to your duties; we will break camp with the dawn.'

Rian turned away and re-entered his tent. He lay awake for the remainder of the night however, the old woman's words echoing through his head. There was no need to send the servants after her; there was nothing either they, or

51

indeed she, could do: it was fated that he would die.

The morning was bright but cold, and with a touch of the fast approaching cold months in the fresh breeze. Rian and his followers set out with the first light of dawn, following the winding track that led through the thick undergrowth and tall trees. The guards were nervous and the animals skittish, and the entire valley seemed to be unusually silent: no morning birds sang, no animals scuttled through the undergrowth, and there was an air – a thick brooding sensation which hung over the little valley like a blanket – which plucked at the nerves and set the senses on edge. Shadows flickered just at the edge of their vision, and the horses shied from pools of darker shadow that edged closer to the track. Some of the more ancient trees seemed to shed a chill miasma, an aura of cold and waiting evil, and Rian started again and again, hearing a cold mocking laughter from afar.

However, towards mid morning the character of the land changed as the track led up and out of the valley. The iciness and the feeling of being watched gradually disappeared, although Rian, standing to one side of the track and watching his people slowly file past, noticed that the entire valley seemed unnaturally shadowed.

They rode westwards, and towards late afternoon left the foothills and entered a broad flat plain bounded on three sides by mountains and the fourth by a dark forest of short stunted trees. As the sun sank into the mountains in the west, Rian and his followers camped in a small natural hollow in the centre of the plain; easily defended and protection of sorts from the ice-tipped breeze that had blown up with evening.

They set their camp for the night in the hollow, with the elderly, the women and children down in the centre and the outer perimeter guarded by a strong force of warriors. This was a strange land – stranger still since they had seen no one throughout the day, and the only living things they had come across were a few solitary birds winging swiftly westwards in the latter half of the evening.

The day darkened swiftly, and storm clouds, which had massed in the north and west for most of the day, rolled across the night sky, obscuring the harshly glittering stars and making the air oppressive.

Rian, touched with a feeling of foreboding, walked to the edge of the hollow, watching, waiting. Occasionally the moon peeked through the clouds, its vacuous face made sinister with strands and wisps of cloud. He started when he imagined the racing clouds formed the face of the dead druid, Bona, and for a moment his last words rumbled across his brain like the sound of distant thunder: *'The water which does not come now will one day find you ... find you ... find you ...'* And then the cloud face dissolved and was gone – and was replaced by the leering face of the old woman in the forest: *'You will not live to see the sun sink again ... water you have kept from me, water shall be your bane ... water be your bane ... your bane ...'.*

Rian grinned mirthlessly. Well, at least he had proved the old woman wrong; he had lived to see the sun sink again, and as for water being his bane ...

Lightning and thunder cracked simultaneously, making him jump; he swore at his own fright and attempted to calm his pounding heart. He turned around and began to run down towards his own tent: soon the heavens would open and there would be a downpour ... and the land needed the water, he decided, stumbling on the hard, dry earth.

By the time he reached the tent it was raining. It wasn't like a normal downpour: the rain fell straight down in a solid mass, striking the hard ground with almost physical force, turning what had been a dry, hard-packed earth only moments before into a wet clinging morass. The ground, dry as it was, swiftly absorbed the water, but it was

53

eventually sated and slowly but surely the water level began to rise.

Rian lay in his tent listening to the drumming of the rain and watching the leather slowly bellying inwards with the weight of the water. Unable to sleep, he prowled the interior of the tent, before eventually pushing out into the rain. The force of the water struck him like a blow, plastering his hair to his head, blinding and deafening him. He stumbled back into the tent and wiped his face, and then crouched in the opening watching the deluge. And then to his right-hand side, one of the tents, unable to bear the weight of the water, collapsed, and then suddenly it seemed as if the whole camp was sinking down into the mud. The fires and torches were gone, doused by the water, and chaos reigned as people stumbled around in the darkness, sliding and falling in the slick earth, trying to find their families or friends. A row of tents collapsed and Rian himself barely escaped being trapped beneath his own as the weight of water folded it in upon itself. The screams of those trapped beneath the tents were drowned out by the frightened cries of the horses and the drumming of the rain. A shout rose briefly above the noise, a cry of warning which was quickly silenced, and then the stampeding horses raced through the hollow, trampling everything in their path in their efforts to reach the higher, drier ground. One struck Rian a glancing blow as it galloped past, sending him crashing backwards. He fell against another person – female by the sound of it – and they both sank into the muck. The woman struggled, kicking and scratching, terrified as liquid muck trickled into her open mouth. Her flailing arm caught Rian across the throat, making him choke. He rose to his knees, and then her knee caught him in the groin, sending him crashing to the ground, retching as the pit of his stomach blossomed fire. He fell face forward onto the ground – and the water and mud were almost over his head. He jerked backwards, pulling his face free of the mire, and then something large and heavy pounded through the mud, spraying him as it went past; there was a terrified scream followed by a sickening wet crunch as the horse trampled the young woman.

Rian attempted to push himself to his feet – and now the water and mud were almost up to his knees ... and still the rain fell unabated.

And then he felt the ground before him tremble, and was aware of a disturbance in the rising water. He heard the snorting and muffled breathing and smelt the terrified horse, and felt the forelegs crash into him ...

The rain continued for the remainder of the night. Out of Rian's five hundred followers barely a score survived – those who had been unlucky enough the night before not to find a space to pitch their tents close to the centre of the hollow and had been forced to camp on the higher ground around the edge. The hollow itself was gone, and there was a small placid lake in its place, its mud-dimmed waters hiding the bodies and artifacts that lay just a little below the surface.

And those few of Rian's followers that had survived rode away into the east and were forgotten, but thereafter the lake was known as Lough Rian ... which time and ignorance has changed to Lough Ree.

Necca awoke with a start. He lay still, his eyes probing the heavy darkness, wondering what had awoken him. He moved slightly, and then he suddenly realised: he was alone in the bed furs, there was no warm breathing body beside him.

'He's dead.' The voice from the darkness was soft, the mearest whisper, and tinged with sorrow. 'I'm sorry, there was nothing else I could do.'

'Ebblue? What's happened?'

A white blur moved before him, and then knelt by his side. He reached out, brushed her breast and then touched her shoulder. 'What has happened?' he repeated softly, aware of a cold chill settling into the pit of his stomach.

'Rian is dead, most of his followers also. The waters have claimed them.'

Necca's fingers tightened briefly on Ebblue's shoulder and then the pressure slackened. '*Sssso*,' he whispered, 'the druid's curse finally caught up with him.'

Strands of fine hair brushed his arm as Ebblue shook her head. 'Your brother was cursed, yes; but Bona never had the power to actually call down his curse. He laid it yes, but he could never call it down. Rian must have been cursed again – and thrice cursed is doomed.'

'Thrice cursed?'

'Your father cursed you both also,' his stepmother reminded him.

'So, I am twice cursed also?'

Ebblue nodded. 'We are all barely this side of destruction,' she said quietly.

'What can we do?' Necca demanded.

Teeth flashed white in the gloom. 'There is nothing you can do... nothing at all.'


Necca, Ebblue and their followers continued on through the pass and followed the track, and towards mid morning they entered the carefully cultivated fields and tended white-sanded roads that led to Brugh na Boine, the abode of Angus Og, the God of Love and the ever-living son of the Dagda.

They rode past strange, slant-eyed, slit-pupilled and deeply tanned creatures who tended the fields or raked the roads. Some raised their long double-jointed fingers in a curious salute or blessing, but others merely regarded them expressionlessly.

Necca reined in his mount and waited until Ebblue rode up beside him. 'What are they?' he asked.

'They are the servants of the De Danann, and some,' she nodded briefly towards a tall, slender figure standing over a dull, lifeless bush, 'have the De Danann blood in them: halflings.' Necca swore softly, for even as he watched the bush began to quiver and tremble, and the dull lifeless leaves changed colour perceptibly, assuming a rich and vibrant hue, and the drooping branches rose to face the sun.

There was a flash of white, startling them both, and then a snow-white dove swooped down from the skies and circled slowly about them, the gentle beat of its wings fanning their faces. It folded its wings and alighted on the head of Ebblue's mount and regarded them for a moment through hard black eyes before taking to the air again and winging south towards the simple white stone walls of Angus' Dun.

'Angus' messenger,' Ebblue explained. 'He is sometimes known as Angus of the Birds; the birds are said to be four kisses that the wind stole from him and transformed into living creatures.'

Necca reined his mount to a halt and watched a white-robed figure leave the dun and walked slowly down the shining road towards them. 'What is this Angus like?' he asked.

'In looks he is said to be very beautiful; a woman's features on a man's skull. But remember,' she warned, 'he is the son of a god – and a god himself in his own right – and he possesses terrible power. His other name is the Disrupter,' she added, and then she leaned across and touched her lover's arm. 'Fear him Necca, fear him, and do not anger him.'

'I fear no man,' Necca said quitely, his voice cold with anger.

'Then you are a fool, Necca MacMarid.' The voice was thin and high, like a pure musical note.

Necca dismounted and walked up to the god. Angus was

tall, a head and more taller than Necca, who was by no means small. His long white robe, somewhat similar to the garment worn by the druids, enveloped his body, but Necca got the impression of leanness, but combined with wiry strength. His face was youthful – almost boyish – beardless and unscarred, and his golden hair was curled close to his skull. But what caught and held Necca's attention were his eyes: they were large and oval, completely dominating his thin face. The pupils were black and flecked with tiny spots of gold that matched his hair and brows... and they were old. They betrayed his great age; his body might not age, the years would never touch it, but his eyes recorded and mirrored his experience. Necca shivered, and for one brief moment saw the image of an old, old man inhabiting the body of a youth through some foul sorcery.

'You should fear me,' Angus said softly, his voice barely above a whisper, yet carrying clearly to all present.

'You are the God of Love,' Necca said sarcastically, 'and why should I fear the God of Love?'

The god smiled. 'There is little love left in you; I see anger and much hate... and fear. And I am only acceptable to those who are at least willing to accept me.' The god paused and added, 'Are you?'

'I want nothing from you,' Necca said quietly, 'but my people are tired; we would wish to rest in these fields for the night, and we will be gone in the morning.'

'No!' Angus shook his head emphatically. 'You cannot stay here.'

Necca stepped closer to the god, and breathed in his raw wild perfume. He rested his hand on his dagger. 'We can go no further,' he said coldly, 'we will stay here.'

Angus turned away, and his words hung delicately on the still air. 'Then on your own head be it.'

Necca's followers camped as far from the white dun as possible, huddling around a few blazing fires, talking quietly, starting at every sound. Necca had doubled and then redoubled the guards around the camp before retiring for the night with Ebblue. But he found the sorceress cold and unresponsive beneath his touch, and when he attempted to hold her she turned away and wrapped her arms around herself. 'Not tonight,' she whispered, 'not here. Can you not feel the Power in the air? What would happen if I were to conceive – what would I bear?' She turned her head to face him and he caught the liquid glint of tears in her eyes. 'We should never have come here, Necca. Angus may be the God of Love, but he is also the Lord of the Birds – and some birds are harbingers of death and eaters of the dead.'

'We will be gone with the dawn,' he soothed her.

'It may be too late then,' she said finally, and turned her head away from him.

Necca was awakened close to dawn by a wild-eyed and terrified guard. The man was almost incoherent with fear and could only drag the half naked prince from his tent and across to the corral where they had left their mounts. Necca pushed his way through the group of silent men and then stood horrified before what remained of their horses. For the animals had been slain – and not only slain, but butchered, mutilated. He remembered what Ebblue had said about Angus being Lord of the Birds: it looked as if some great raven had torn out each animal's entrails and then picked at the flesh ... and, significantly, all the animals' eyes had been plucked out.

He breathed deeply, quelling his rising gorge. 'Did anyone hear anything ... see anything?' he demanded.

The guards shook their heads. 'It was sorcery, my lord,' one said.

'Aye, sorcery,' another agreed.

'What will we do now?' another asked.

Necca turned away from the carnage and pushed his way through the guards. 'There is nothing we can do – except talk to the god,' he spat.

Angus was waiting for him when he returned to his tent.

59

Ebblue was sitting up in a corner, the thick furs pulled up to her chin, shivering visibly, her eyes wide with fear. Necca could almost taste the strangeness in the air, and he assumed that this was the Power she had spoken of the night before. It was sharp and flat, like the air before a storm, and his skin began to tingle as if a host of insects were swarming over it.

'You killed my animals,' he accused, walking around the god and kneeling by Ebblue's side. 'Are you all right?' he asked her.

She nodded and clung to him.

'I warned you not to stay,' Angus said.

'And I told you we would.'

'This is a strange and dangerous land,' Angus said. 'It is not the land you know – you have passed beyond your own fields and partly into the Shadowland, and all manner of creatures stalk these lands at night,' he added quietly.

'You killed my animals,' Necca stated flatly, 'and unless we find fresh mounts, then I am afraid we must stay here.'

The god nodded and his old eyes hooded over in a smile. 'That is why I am here; I have come to offer you mounts, or at least,' he added slowly, 'a mount.'

Necca rose from Ebblue's side. 'A mount? You have come to offer us one miserable horse! Well, you can take your horse . . .'

'This is not an ordinary horse,' the god said calmly. 'It cannot be ridden; the man has not yet been born that can tame him, but it will act as a beast of burden.'

'God,' Necca snapped, 'we had twenty beasts carrying our belongings – your one horse is not likely to make much difference is it?'

'You must wait and see,' Angus said with a smile. He bowed shortly, turned and slipped through the tent flaps.

Necca sank down beside Ebblue. He found himself trembling with anger and frustration; he felt like a child struggling against a parent: there was nothing he could do –

and he knew it. His stepmother put her arms around him and pulled his head onto her breast, and then she held him while he wept.

It might have been a horse. At some time in the dim and distant past its ancestors might have been of the equine breed, but now...

The creature stood about fifteen hands high – which was normal – but about four times the length of a normal horse! It was eight-legged, and at least two men could have sat side by side on its back. Its head was broad and flat, more reminiscent of a bull's than that of a horse, and just beneath its large rounded ears were tiny stub horns. Its eyes were flat and yellow, slit-pupilled like a cat's and its teeth were sharp and pointed... and Necca wondered what meat this creature ate. Its coat was smooth and glossy and tinged with a metallic green, and its hooves were cloven, like a goat's.

The prince turned to the god. 'What abomination is this?'

The god smiled. 'It is a whim... a minor indulgence,' he smiled again. 'But it will carry all your belongings without tiring. However, a warning: do not allow anyone to mount the beast, for to do so would be fatal... and not only to the rider I fear. Secondly, once the creature begins to move, it must be kept moving, and on no account must it be allowed to stop.'

'Why?' Necca demanded.

The god smiled, the corners of his lips curving upwards, but his eyes remaining cold and hard. 'You disobeyed me and spent the night in my domain. You will never again spend any length of time in any one place; you are doomed to wander for the rest of your days. You see,' Angus said conversationally, 'I too have cursed you. Oh, I know you have been cursed twice, and now I am adding my curse to that. But to discover the curse, you must first allow the creature to stop.'

61

'And you are the God of Love?' Necca said slowly.

'I am what you make of me,' Angus said, turning away.

Necca and his followers departed close to mid morning, the strange beast loaded down with their belongings. The creature moved uncomplainingly in a plodding steady movement, and responded to blows on either shoulder to make it turn. With onset of evening they camped in a small stand of trees and Necca, mindful of Angus' warning, detailed a group of his men to walk the creature around the camp again and again until dawn, when they set out again, moving north and eastwards this time. They continued on for ten days, their pace necessarily slow, dictated by the plodding of the beast which was not much faster than a man's walk. Necca's warriors naturally fretted at this slow pace and some foraged ahead, seeking a suitable camping spot. Towards the afternoon of the tenth day, they returned with news of a broad flat plain ahead, dotted with stands of stunted trees.

They reached the plain towards late evening, when the shadows were beginning to lengthen into night, and even Necca had to admit it was perfect. The flat plain – although affording no natural protection – meant that no one could approach them undetected, and once the trees were cleared there would be enough wood to construct a large fort.

And so they made their way downwards onto the grasslands, and it was here that Necca made his first grievous mistake. The plain had possibilities; properly protected and with a fresh supply of water the land could be worked to produce at least one – and possibly two – good harvests. However, while the prince was taken up with his plans for the future, the creature was allowed to stop moving...

He had rotated the drivers regularly, but even so the task of guiding a slow moving beast, which at the same time both terrified and awed, quickly grew boring, and now, with the end of their journey in sight, the drivers grew lax, until for one moment they forgot to drive the creature.

It stopped.

Ebblue screamed a warning and, calling upon her powers, sent a bright needle-sharp jab of fire in its direction. The glittering point struck the animal in its hindquarters, jolting it into movement again. But the damage had already been done. The ground beneath where the beast had stopped had abruptly grown wet and marshy, and now a bubbling pool sprang forth. The gurgling water began to fountain upwards, growing higher and higher. Necca threw himself forward onto the water, trying to press it down with his body. He could feel the chill liquid immediately soaking through his jerkin; he could feel the pressure against his chest, pumping and pulsating like a heartbeat; he could feel it pushing upwards, could feel it growing stronger. And then in a sudden gush it carried him upwards, lifting him completely off his feet and tossing him to one side. The water rose in a long slender pillar, fountaining up into the darkening night sky, catching the last of the sun's rays, cresting into a fine rainbow-hued spray.

Necca scrambled to his feet – and immediately slipped and fell in the mud. The hard ground was sinking. And then Ebblue was by his side, her hands moving quickly, her slender fingers tracing intricate patterns in the damp evening air. She cried out in a strange wailing accent, the words rising and falling with the pulsating of the water. And then her words began to slow, and as they did so, so did the water. Soon she was only whispering – and the gushing water had fallen to the merest trickle. She knelt in the muddy earth and placed both hands flat across the puncture in the ground – a puncture in the shape of a cloven hoof – and the water stopped.

Necca helped Ebblue to her feet, and gently scraped most of the muck from her hands, and although his own hands were trembling, his stepmother's were as steady as a rock.

'The spell will last a day and a night,' she said, a little

breathlessly. 'You must have a wall built around it, and then I'll transfer the spell of containment to the stones of the wall, and that will hold it.'

'Was that Angus' curse?' Necca asked quietly, still shaken by the suddenness of it all.

The sorceress nodded.

And then the prince smiled. 'Then, we have beaten him – we've tricked him. His spell has been used – and yet we still live.'

'Unless we cover this water hole,' Ebblue said quickly, 'his spell may still claim us.'

By the afternoon of the following day the well hole had been covered in; smooth stones covering the actual hole, and then a low wall built around that, roofed and with a round wooden door bolted into the stone. Ebblue transferred her spell of containment into the stones of the wall and the ground it covered, but adjusted the wording of the spell so that the door might be lifted thrice in every day, but for no more than twenty-one heartbeats – so that water might be drawn off. Necca then had a small round beehive-shaped hut built around the wall and over the well, and installed an old woman, Marue, whose husband had been lost early on in the journey, as the well keeper, and it was her task to ensure that the well was kept locked and covered at all times, and only opened for the time specified.

And so Necca and his followers settled on the Plain of the Grey Copse around the magic well, and there they prospered, for even in times of drought the well never ran dry, nor during the hardest winter did it freeze over.

And the years passed.

Ebblue bore Necca two daughters: Aeru and Liban. She survived the birth of her second daughter by barely a month but, weakened by years of hardship and the constant use of her powers to renew the spell of containment, and having to call forth the crops from the land and turn aside the worst of the storms that might have shattered the small community, she died and was laid to rest beside the well.

As they grew towards maturity the two girls began to resemble their parents: Aeru favouring her father and Liban bearing a startling resemblance to her mother, and also touched with her mother's powers and capable of small magics.

In time Aeru married Curan, a stranger who had wandered into their camp late one evening, wild-eyed and ranting of great *peist* – a serpent – that had pursued him. Aeru had nursed him back to health, but his wits had been addled, or perhaps the cold breath of ancient sorcery had touched him, for his eyes were thereafter wild and seeking, and in night's darkest hours he would often start from his bed, shouting and crying out, pointing at creatures only he could see. But Aeru came to love the strange, gentle and caring poet and married him – even though his nickname about the camp was 'the Simpleton'.

But it was the Simpleton who first predicted the well's overflowing.

It was a warm summer evening and the air was heavy and humid, seeming to press down on the hard dry earth. The evening was hushed with no birds singing or calling and no wind rustling the long grass. The sun had dipped down behind the trees to the west, but the rounded tops were still touched with bronze and ochre fire. The People of the Well – as Necca and his followers had come to be known – were gathered around Curan who sat easily on a low tree stump regaling them with a tale of Erin's ancient past, a tale of the coming of the first invaders to the tiny island: wild warrior women from the far and mysterious east. They sat enthralled as the Simpleton engaged them with words and images, calling forth the pictures of the savage beast-men as they attacked the caves of the Caesirians, and then drawing down the tragedy as the easterners succumbed to the final deadly plague, the ultimate fate of many of Erin's early invaders. He finished his tale in a whisper, and the only sound in the still night air was the sobbing of a young woman as she imagined the tiny eastern sorceress toppling into the waves as the huge funeral fire stained the sky behind her.

Curan smiled as he finished his tale and the light of madness began to burn in his eyes. 'And now that I have told you of the past, would you like me to tell you of the future?' He grinned broadly, and those nearest him drew back, for if touched he was capable of great violence during these fits. 'But what's this I see?' he asked in a hushed and wondering voice. 'Why, the end of the Caesirians is not that much different from the fate of the People of the Well.'

'What do you see, Curan?' Necca asked quietly, tiredly. The years had not been kind to him. The prince was greyed and bowed, and touched with a heaviness of spirit that nothing could ever lift, and only seemed to lighten in the presence of his daughters, and especially Liban.

'I see death, prince,' the Simpleton mocked. 'I see death . . . and in a fashion I can see life. Life and death . . . life and death,' he began to chant in a singsong voice.

'What sort of death?' the prince demanded, aware of the growing murmurs of unease behind him.

Curan looked across at the well hut with its tiny ever-lit torch flickering over the door. 'A wet death,' he said, and fell into a fit of giggling. Necca turned and searched the crowd, and then, catching sight of his daughter, nodded to her and then to her husband. Aeru came forward and gently lifted Curan from the tree stump. The crowd moved back as they passed, afraid to help her carry the drooling man, knowing that he could bear no touch but hers.

Necca stared after them, something like the old fear beginning to seep back into his bones and the cold knot beginning to form at the pit of his stomach. For he knew then, he knew with an absolute certainty, that the gods could never be cheated . . . and that thrice cursed was doomed.

*

For some weeks thereafter the well was guarded with extra vigilance, because, for all Curan's rantings, his prophecies in the past had proved uncannily accurate and it was generally accepted that he had the Sight. But as time passed the extra guards were drafted to other duties, for it was now harvesting time, and every hand was needed to bring in the crop before the raiders and bandits came. And so old Marue was left alone once more in the small dark hut, with no company but the gurgling and trickling of waters inside the round covered well. Sometimes it spoke to her.

It had begun as a whispering at first, the merest thread of imagined sound. She had doubted it of course; a woman alone day and night should expect to hear strange and unusual noises, and of course, she was no longer young, and age played strange tricks on the mind. But the sound continued, whispering her name, calling her, calling... calling...

And soon she began to lie across the flat well cover, her ear pressed against the cold damp wood, listening. She could hear the voice of her husband, and sometimes of her children: both the children she had and those she had thought she might have but which never came... they all lived within the waters of the well.

And the voices begged for release.

But the well could only be opened three times in any one day: at sunrise, when the first rays of the morning sun touched the tip of the round hut; at noon, when the hut cast no shadow; and at sunset when the hut's long shadow raced darkly across the ground.

The well cover could only be left off for the space of twenty-one heartbeats, and over the years Marue had grown expert at counting the beats. At first she had held her own wrist and counted the pulse, but then she realised that excitement might rob them of valuable time for drawing the much needed water if her pulse were speeded up, or sickness could cause a fatal error if her pulse were slow. And so now she usually counted steadily while three young girls drew the water up in large pails and poured it into the barrels that were kept in the hut for that purpose.

On the last fine day for harvesting the girls were early for the noon drawing, and they disturbed Marue who was deep in conversation with her long dead husband, Rael. He was pleading for release, begging her to free him from the cold, so cold water...

The old woman came to her feet quickly, hearing the girlish laughter just outside the closed door. One of the girls tapped loudly, and then pushed it open and stepped into the room. She stopped just inside the threshold, allowing her eyes to adjust to the darkness.

'Marue? Marue... Oh, there you are. How can you bear it so dark in here?'

'It's the light, my dear; when you get to my age the light burns your eyes. Is it time?'

'Almost.' One of the girls stood by the door watching the last vestiges of shadow disappear beneath the glare of the sun. 'Now!'

The two girls pulled away the cover and began to draw off the water as quickly as possible; Marue immediately began to keep count.

'*One... two... three...*'

Her husband wasn't in there, she knew that. Her husband had died on the road here, coughing out his lungs with a chill caught walking around the perimeter of the camp one damp night.

'*...four... five... six...*'

He had died, choking on his own blood, and you might say Necca killed him, and hadn't Necca been cursed in the first place? They were mad to have followed him. And what right did he have to bring them all this way –

'*...seven... eight... nine...*'

– if he had been cursed; and thrice cursed at that. By father, druid and god. He was doomed. He was a walking

68

dead man, and he had killed her husband as surely as if he had driven a dagger into his heart.

'...ten... eleven... twelve...'

And now her husband lay dead beneath the cold, dark water, trapped forever by Ebblue's spell. And what of her children? They too lay trapped beneath the waters.

'...ten... eleven... twelve...'

What about her two sons who had died when Necca's father had warred with the neighbouring tribes? And what about her daughter – the daughter that had cost her her womb – who had been stolen when Miridach, King of Ulster, had come raiding four – or was it five? – seasons ago? They had killed her, probably raped her also, but they had certainly killed her, for she now lived beneath the waters and whispered late at night to her mother about the cold, cold water.

'...thirteen... fourteen... fifteen... sixteen... seventeen... eighteen...'

One of the girls glanced across at the old woman in alarm. The old woman's lips were still moving silently in a count. But Gael had been drawing the water now for three seasons, and she knew – *she knew!* – something was wrong, for the old woman had only reached eighteen, and yet *she* had already counted twenty-one!

Her scream was lost as the pent-up water erupted upwards in a solid pillar that ripped through the roof, scattering the rounded stones and ragged bodies across the flat plain. The rest of the hut blew outwards, the stones scything through the men, women and children caught in their path. They were the lucky ones.

The ground opened out in a great V-shaped cut that spewed water upwards as it raced across the ground – and then the land abruptly sank. The two arms of the V swung around and joined, and the oval of land between them dropped downwards and was engulfed in the rising water, and over the shouts and cries rose the exultant wailing of the released water, crying out its release.

And in a matter of twenty heartbeats the entire Plain of the Grey Copse sank down beneath the water, the whole community wiped out in an instant, and when the dust and grit and water had settled, where there had once been a green and fertile plain was now only a broad flat lake. The poets and travellers called it Lough Necca, but time and ignorance has changed that to Lough Neagh, the largest lake in the islands of Britain and Ireland.


## II – THE MERMAID

Liban, Necca's daughter first heard the screams, and then chunks of rock ploughed into the ground by her feet. She looked up and saw the seemingly solid pillar of water rising straight up into the noonday air, sunlight sparkling and glinting in rainbow hues making it a thing of beauty ... until she saw the bodies and realised what had happened. For a single heartbeat the pillar faltered, and then Liban was thrown to the ground by a hammer blow. She attempted to climb to her feet, but the very ground itself was shaking, trembling violently ... and then it shifted.

Liban saw the sheer cliffs rear up all around her, the sky was blotted out by shifting clouds of dust, and a grey wall of water rose up ... and slowly it began to topple down towards her.

The young woman stared at it for a shocked moment, and then she plunged her hands deep into the soft earth, calling up what little she remembered of her mother's lore and her own natural talent. Her throat worked, shaping words and phrases that were already ancient when the world was young, drawing forth the very magic of the land itself.

And the crashing wall of water toppled and fell ...

Liban flung up her hands – and the water stopped barely a hand's breadth from her face! The grey-black water exploded in a frenzy against the invisible wall, and then flowed over and around the tiny bubble of force with which she had surrounded herself. And so she sat there, secure, while all around her the water rose and indistinct shapes, murky in the filth, brushed against the force wall; and sometimes they assumed definite shapes and peered inwards with staring eyes and cried out with open mouths. Liban trembled as the figures attempted to claw their way in; she knew they were the corpses of her people, but the water seemed to give them a strange life . . . and at times it seemed as if they *were* alive. But as the afternoon wore on, and the lighter coloured surface of the water disappeared upwards into the distance and darkness closed in, Liban, already exhausted with the effort of calling up the earth magic, fell into a troubled and fitful sleep.

When she awoke it was pitch black and she was cold. For a moment she stared around wildly, disorientated by the absolute darkness and the complete absence of sound: where were the muted shouts of the guards, and the crackling of the camp fires, and the children's shouts and cries . . .?

Memory returned, and with it terror. She was trapped here, and the Dagda only knew how far she was beneath the surface of the water. She couldn't drop the force wall, for the very pressure of the water would surely crush her, and yet she couldn't survive here for very much longer; already the air tasted sharp and caught at the back of her throat. Besides, she had no food and – she began to laugh hysterically – she had no water . . . *no water* . . .

She dug her long nails into the palm of her hand drawing blood, the pain shocking her back to reality. If she allowed the madness of fear to overcome her, then death would surely follow. If only she had some light.

The young woman raised her hands and touched her face.

She breathed onto the palms before bringing her long fingers together, and then she lowered her head and called upon her inner strength. Light blossomed at the tips of her fingers. It was faint and tenuous and pulsed in time with her heartbeat, but Liban poured more of her strength into the tiny glowing ball and it gradually grew and swelled until she could cup it in the palms of both hands. The glowing ball was pure and white, tinged with the merest trace of emerald since Liban had called upon the earth magic earlier. It shed its cold light all around her ... but there was nothing to see. No fish swam in the depths of the water, no creatures scuttled under the stones and even the whirling corpses had disappeared. The water was dead, and it would take many years for life to seed itself in its cold depths. Liban raised the globe of light above her head, but she could still see nothing, only the edges of the blackness as it retreated before the light.

And so she was trapped; there was no escape – at least in her own form.

The thought hit her like a physical blow, the shock numbing her. It was horrible, too horrible to even think about.

But as the day – or was it night? – wore on, the thought returned and began to whisper insidiously within her head. She was trapped ... trapped ... trapped ... The word beat inside her until she wanted to scream and scream and scream. She struggled against the madness that clustered around her, tainting her thoughts like the very tainted air she was now breathing. If she didn't make a decision soon, then she would be dead: the air couldn't last much longer and already she was breathing in her own poisons.

And of course there was no real answer. If she remained where she was, then she would die; if she dropped the force wall, then she was dead, but if she changed her shape? And if she survived, then what would be the price? To assume a form that could survive in the cold waters of the lake was possible, but to reassume her own form was another thing entirely, and she doubted if she did effect the first transformation whether she would have either the strength or power left to accomplish the second.

But there was no choice.

Liban stripped off her clothing, folding it in a neat bundle by her side, although she knew she would never use it again. She then lay down on the soft, damp ground and spread her legs to touch the force wall with either foot, and her hands stretched out to touch cold fingers against it on either side. She closed her eyes and allowed the darkness to close in and take her, and with the darkness came the fragments of dreams and old nightmares. Liban allowed the images to slip and flow across her closed lids . . . until she caught at one and held it. She concentrated on the nightmare image, calling it forth from the very depths of her mind, adding in details, visualising it in its entirety. And then she began to add to it, gradually overlaying her own image onto the picture she had built up, until in her mind they became one and the same.

She opened her eyes. The small bubble of force was bright with silver ghost fire, the residue of her Power, illuminating her slim body in delicate metallic shades. Liban raised her head slightly and looked down at her body, past her small breasts and the swell of her stomach . . . and then she began to draw upon the last of her waning strength.

What seemed like silver dust motes began to gather on her legs, reflecting and refracting the dim light, blinding her. Soon her legs from her groin downwards were bathed in a luminous sheet of darting light, and she felt the numbness creeping upwards from her toes, rising . . . rising . . . rising, slowly engulfing her.

When she awoke her head was pounding and throbbing, her throat was raw and coated and her eyes were streaming. She breathed in the foul air and choked, and then struggled to sit up. But her feet were dead and she couldn't feel her legs. It was dark within the bubble, the ghost light was gone, but she managed to throw a dim shadow-light along her fingers... and she saw.

The spell had worked: she was no longer fully human. She had successfully transferred her nightmare image to reality, and now she wore no legs; they were gone and in their place a gleaming scaled fish-tail flapped against the ground. There had been other changes also: her fingers had grown an extra flap of skin between them and a membrane had closed across her nose, and beneath her chin on her throat were two semi-circular serrated openings: primitive gills. A light scattering of scales dusted her body, and her soft breasts had firmed and hardened.

Liban held the light for a long time, examining the changes in her body through the tears which misted her eyes, and then she allowed the light to die, repulsed at what she had become. In the darkness she sat up and traced an arcane pattern against the invisible wall, allowing the earth's forces to slip back into the damp ground. Water seeped in from under the edges of the weakened wall, quickly covering the fish-tail and beginning to creep up her naked body. She didn't feel the chill, and could only feel the water's pressure as a gentle push. She breathed deeply and held her breath as the water rose up over her mouth and across her eyes. Her vision blurred and then cleared, and she was conscious that she was no longer holding her breath. She opened her mouth – and nothing happened, although she could feel a cold gentle susurration in the sides of her throat as the gills worked. The water took her then, lifting her buoyantly upwards, and she rode the still turbulent water, practising manipulating the fish-tail, but rising towards the lightening water at the same time.

Liban broke the surface, and felt the skin cease flapping on her throat; her mouth worked, and she was suddenly breathing normally again. Her vision blurred as something slipped across her eyes, and then she could see clearly. She saw the broad flat surface of the newly formed lake, black now in the night, but silver-touched with moonlight, speckled with the hard points of light from the stars. And then she wept; she wept for the beauty she now saw, and the beauty that was lost forever beneath it; she wept for her father and sister and her people. She wept for herself; what she had been and what she had now become.


Beoc sent the small round currach skimming across the flat waters of the lake, lost in thought, muscles working automatically. He was still slightly stunned by the Abbot's decision to send him – *him!* – to Rome to bear the missive that Congall, Abbot of Bangor, had drawn up, into the very hands of the Pope himself. It was ... it was an honour, and the young monk shouted for joy. And something answered him.

Beoc started and caught a crab, the oar cutting into the water, catching and then suddenly coming free, tumbling him back into the tiny wood and hide craft. It tilted dangerously, spinning around and shipping some water.

The young man sat up carefully in the small craft and listened intently, sweat beginning to glisten on his already balding head. Someone – something – had answered him; it wasn't an echo.

The boat rocked gently on the waters of the lake while the young monk bailed out the water with cupped hands. And then a long sharp *V* suddenly sliced through the water towards him. Beoc froze, and stared at the white water, entranced. Across the water in Scotland there were tales of great *peisti* – serpents – in some of the older lakes, but there were no snakes in Ireland, not since Saint Patrick had driven them out. But what then could it be? The young monk poked into the water with the oar ... and it was abruptly snatched from his grasp, almost pulling him in with it. He cried out, calling on God for protection... and then a head broke the surface of the water.

It was the head of a young woman, her black-green hair plastered wetly to her head, her small dark eyes blinking rapidly. Her mouth moved once and then she spoke in a curiously flat accent, using an archaic mode of speech. 'I am sorry, I did not mean to startle you.'

Beoc looked around. He was almost in the centre of the huge lake, many miles from either shore... and yet, where was this young woman's craft?

She came up out from the water, her shoulders and then her breasts breaking the surface, and she clung to the side of the currach for support, tilting it dangerously. Beoc glanced down at her hands – and he suddenly knew: they were webbed!

The young man crossed himself. 'You... you are a sea-maid?' he asked in a small voice.

'So I have been called,' she replied softly, her vowels clipped, her speech broken, as if she had not spoken for many years.

Beoc scooped a handful of water from the bottom of his craft, blessed it, and then threw it over the maid. She blinked and tossed her head, scattering fine droplets in every direction. However she did not scream or cry out when the water touched her: she was therefore no demon. 'Who are you?' Beoc asked quietly.

The young woman lay back in the water and Beoc caught a glimpse of a green-gold tail undulating gently beneath the surface of the water. 'I am Liban,' she said slowly, 'once daughter of Necca and Ebblue, who walked this land some three hundred and more of your years ago.'

'Necca and Ebblue! But they are myths; this lake is called after Necca... Lough Necca.'

'He was my father.' The mermaid smiled at the young monk's confusion. 'Oh, but do not think I always wore this

76

form; listen and I will tell you my tale...'

And as the currach drifted slowly across the broad lake, Liban swam alongside relating to Beoc the tale of the thrice cursed brothers, her witch-mother and the final enchantment that had rendered her into her present form.

It was close to evening when the small craft beached on the eastern side of the lake. Beoc shook his head attempting to clear his mind of the visions the young woman had woven, of a time when the One-God had still not come to Erin's shores, a time when the old gods held sway, a time of power and enchantment, a time of magic. 'Will I see you again?' he asked her suddenly.

'Do you wish to see me again?' she said shyly.

'I do.'

Liban smiled. 'I will meet you a year and a day from today on that stretch of water called Inver Ollamh in the east.'

Beoc laughed. 'You know no one is going to believe me,' he called out as the mermaid drifted slowly out into the darkening waters.

'Bring them with you,' she laughed, 'but promise me you'll be there,' she added.

'Oh, I'll be there,' the monk swore as the dark-haired head slipped without a sound beneath the flat black waters of the lake.


'Father Abbot, you cannot!' Beoc demanded.

'Brother, you forget yourself,' Congall reminded the younger man quietly. 'It seems your journey to the Holy City not only broadened your outlook, but also taught you some of their ill manners.'

Beoc looked wildly around the shores of the little inlet at the monks preparing thick nets and taking up positions with long pointed gaffs by the waterside. 'Father, a year ago she promised me she would come here of her own free will. She will come,' he said insistently, 'but she is not a ... a ...'

77

'A what, my son?' the abbot said gently. The older man took the young monk's arm and led him aside. 'My son, she is a sorry creature. If your story is true – and I must admit I have checked the facts and they seem to bear out her tale – then she is possibly the last of the followers of the Old Faith – and trapped in an unholy body that is neither beast nor man. But a body,' he continued, 'fashioned by the most foul sorcery. And while she might be able to survive in this unnatural form, her eternal soul is trapped, trapped in the body of one of the damned ... and it is crying out for release. We have a calling – no, a duty – to try and carry the Word of the Risen Christ to her, to try and release her from her sentence and bring her into the bosom of the Church.'

'And if she doesn't want to be brought into the bosom of the Church?' Beoc asked quietly.

The abbot looked at the younger man in shocked amazement. 'Brother, it seems we must talk at some length when this sorry episode is finished. Such thoughts are heresy. Perhaps the sea-maid enchanted you ...'

'Only her innocence enchanted me.'

'Aaah, you see! You may have renounced the lusts of the flesh, but they can still attempt to claim us. They are the sendings of the Evil One. Tell me my son, have you thought of this maid over the past year?'

'Often.'

The abbot smiled triumphantly, but said nothing.

About mid morning the smooth surface of the inlet was disturbed by a long foaming line of water that cut directly across the lake towards where Beoc waited, sitting on a low stone, his head buried in his hands. Some of the monks noticed the disturbance and brought it to the attention of the abbot, but he only nodded silently, and indicated that they should return to their positions.

The black-green-haired head broke the surface, and hard black eyes regarded Beoc for a moment. 'Why so silent, holy man?' she asked in her strange accent.

The young monk started and looked up. He quickly glanced to either side. 'Quickly, you must flee, you cannot stay here. Go ... go!' He ran down into the shallows and attempted to push the mermaid away.

Liban resisted him. 'What is the matter; I thought ...'

'It's the abbot,' Beoc explained in a rush, 'he wants to capture you, to set you up as an example of what will happen to those who follow the Old Faith, of how it will eventually pervert and destroy them. There are monks here to ...'

The young monk yelped in surprise as he was roughly grabbed from behind and thrown to the ground. He had a brief glimpse of brown-robed bodies rushing past him and then he heard the shouts and screams ...

The first monk to reach Liban paused momentarily at the sight of her bare breasts; he closed his eyes and crossed himself – and then something crashed into his legs, sending him toppling backwards into the arms of another monk. They both went down in a flurry of arms and legs, kicking and struggling in the chill water. But now other arms were reaching for the mermaid. Her fluked tail swept out catching one high in the chest, lifting him off his feet and throwing him backwards. The tail then flipped back and snapped across another's face, snapping teeth, jaw and nose in one fluid movement. One grabbed Liban's arm – and shouted in surprise as his grip slid along her scaled flesh. Her webbed fingers caught his hair and pulled him down, plunging his head beneath the water. His shout ended in a gurgle. Another leaped across the fallen monk with a net in his hands. Liban's tail swept up and caught him between the legs, doubling him up, and then her tail hit him again, striking upwards and into his face, propelling him back onto the beach. But now there were monks coming from all sides. Liban thrashed and struggled; her webbed fingers tipped with long, slightly curving nails tore flesh and gouged eyes before they were finally caught, and her tail broke limbs and ribs, cracked skulls and flattened faces before it was entangled in a lead-weighted net.

They carried her – still struggling – to the shore where Congall stood, a vial of holy water in one hand and a cross in the other. He blessed her, scattered some of the holy water over her and proceeded to intone the ritual for the dismissal of spirits. Liban gradually quietened and lay on the rough sand watching him intently. When he was finished she smiled and spoke in her flat and broken voice. 'Holy man, you remind me of a druid my father once told me about; he too was an arrogant, ignorant man.'

Congall smiled benevolently. 'I forgive you of course, my child.'

Liban spat. 'I do not want your forgiveness, all I want is my freedom.'

'But you will never be free while you are trapped in that ... body, and are ignorant of the One True God.' The abbot turned away. 'Take her to the abbey.'

'Hold!'

Congall turned slowly. 'What is it you want Fergus?' he asked, a hard note creeping into his voice.

The speaker was a huge man, standing a head and shoulders above the rest of the monks. He regarded the abbot from clear grey eyes, and when he spoke his speech was slow and measured. 'Am I to take it that you are claiming this maid?'

Congall looked surprised. 'But of course, why not? She has been taken in my domain.'

'Aaah, but I actually held her,' Fergus said. 'While your monks were being battered about like birds in a strong breeze, I alone held her.'

'That sounds suspiciously like pride in your voice,' the abbot snapped.

'And is that anger I hear in yours?' Fergus asked. 'And do you not want the maid so that you can go down in history as the first abbot since Patrick to convert one of the Old Folk to the Way? Is that not pride?'

80

'The mermaid belongs to no one,' Beoc said suddenly, 'she is free – and has been free for three hundred years. She came here of her own free will to see me – *me!* And now will you all leave her alone,' he shouted.

'Beoc, as your abbot I command you to be silent,' Congall said.

The young monk rounded on the older man. 'If you continue, then you will find that you are no longer my abbot. I once respected you – aye, honoured and even loved you – but I am quickly coming to loathe you,' he spat.

'Brothers... brothers... brothers...' Niall, one of the oldest monks came between them, his hands raised. 'What are you doing? What has happened to you? Can you not recognise the hand of Satan amongst you?' The old monk turned to the abbot. 'You have claimed the maid, you wish to convert her to the Way, and that is worthy... but are the reasons behind it worthy?'

The old man then turned to Fergus without waiting for an answer from the abbot. 'And you brother, why do you want the maid? What will you do with her, for look, she cannot be used in the manner of women even if we were not sworn to celibacy. Would you just keep her so that you could say, "*Look, I caught the mermaid of Lough Necca?*"' The old monk slowly shook his head and looked across at Beoc. 'And you my son, why do you want the maid?'

'I don't want her,' Beoc said quietly, 'she is not mine. I wished to talk with her, nothing more. But if I could have her now, then I would surely set her free.'

Niall smiled toothlessly and then turned back to the abbot. 'Let us not dispute the matter today. Let us rest and tend to our wounded. Tomorrow is the Sabbath, and surely we will have our answer then?'

'And what about me?' Liban asked quietly.

The old monk knelt painfully by the mermaid's side. 'You, I fear, must remain with us until the morn. But you must not fret,' he added gently, 'the night will bring many things: the cool air clears heads, the darkness aids thoughts, and the night brings dreams...'

The dream was the same for the three holy men. They were each standing alone by a lakeside on a moonlit night. The sky was clear and the surface of the water by their feet was smooth. Suddenly the water shifted and rippled, and the mermaid rose from the sea in a gilded chariot drawn by two snow-white oxen. The chariot then raced up the beach and cut across country. Each monk followed until he came to a crossroads. He could hear the chariot approaching in the distance ... and he could also hear the approach of the other two monks. He cut down one of the roads and waited for the chariot ...

In Congall's dream the ox-drawn chariot carried the girl to him.

And for Fergus the mermaid was brought to him.

And in Beoc's dream the oxen carried Liban to him.

Niall supervised the loading of the chariot, ensuring that the mermaid was comfortable, and that the oxen were securely yoked together. And then, followed by the rest of the monks from the monastery, he led the oxen to the nearest crossroads.

The three claimants to the mermaid had arrived earlier and taken up positions on the road. Straight down one arm of the crossroads Congall knelt by the side of the road, his hands clasped in prayer. To the right Fergus busied himself weeding a patch around a small roadside shrine, and to the left Beoc sat with his back against a stone, reading a precious handwritten copy of the Book.

Niall walked the beasts around in a circle and then he moved away. The oxen continued to circle aimlessly for a while and then they broke out of the rut and moved off ...

down the left hand path, towards Beoc.

The young monk looked up at the sound of hooves. The mermaid smiled down at him. 'I never doubted,' he said quietly.

'Neither did I,' Liban said, as he gently lifted her down from the chariot and then carried her across the fields and down onto the beach towards the waves.

And there they talked long into the morning, whilst back at the crossroads Congall and Fergus argued with Niall. And when they finally reached the young monk and the mermaid, they found Beoc reading to her from the Book, and Liban silently weeping.

The monks gathered around in a circle and sat listening to Beoc. Fergus turned to Congall with awe in his voice. 'It is a long time since I heard anyone weep to hear the word of the Lord.'

The abbot nodded. 'There is a lesson here for all of us.'

And when Beoc had finished, and the sun was sinking into the west, Liban turned to him and said, 'You must baptise me into your faith.'

'But . . . are you sure? You know so little about it . . .'

'But you believe in it?' Liban persisted.

Beoc nodded.

'You believe in it strongly enough to foreswear your family, a wife and children of your own?'

Again Beoc nodded. 'My faith is my family, the church my love.'

'It must be a fine faith to attract devotion such as yours.'

'It is,' Beoc whispered, and all around him the monks nodded silently.

'Then baptise me,' Liban insisted.

'But listen to me,' Beoc said desperately. 'If I baptise you then your spell will be broken, you will regain your own form and age will once again claim you; you will die.'

Liban nodded. 'I know.' And then she added, 'All I ask is that when I die I will be laid to rest in your own grave.'

Beoc nodded, blinking back the sudden sting of tears.

The mermaid smiled. 'Then begin...'

'Are you sure?' Beoc whispered.

'Begin!' Liban commanded.

'I baptise you in the Name of the Father... and of the Son... and of the Holy Ghost...'

# Chapter Three

# THE WOLF MAIDS

The sunlight lingered briefly in the mouth of the cave, gradually turning from a pale bronze to a deep purple, briefly flaring red before sinking into the Western Ocean. The night stars – which had already claimed the sky to the east – began to glitter in the salmon and rose coloured sky above the sunset, their harsh brilliance still dull and muted. A few seabirds called plaintively before settling down on the white-streaked cliffs, and soon the only sound was the hissing of the sea on the sands far, far below and the whisper of the breeze through the tough razor-edged grass.

And in the mouth of the cave a shadow moved, and large oval points of light glittered briefly amber before blinking out.

Giolla awoke suddenly when he heard the panic-stricken bleatings of the newly born lambs. Remaining in the shadow of the standing stones, he knuckled the sleep from his eyes and peered down the valley. He could see the white moving shapes of the sheep milling about, but nothing else: there were no horses, no sounds of metal on metal, no shouts, no flaring torches. The young man fitted an egg-shaped stone into his sling and, swinging it slowly, moved as quietly as possible down into the valley. A long low dark shape moved across the whiteness of the sheep and Giolla instinctively loosed his slingshot. The hard stone struck something soft and he heard a muted yelp. Dogs!

85

And then the night was split asunder by a bone-chilling howl, freezing the young man in his tracks. It was immediately answered by another, and yet another. Not dogs – *wolves!*

Giolla's fingers trembled as he attempted to fit another stone into the leather sling, and he dropped it. He could hear the creatures moving now, could hear their hoarse panting, and then the sudden scream of a slaughtered lamb cut through him. He had another stone fitted and the sling was buzzing around his head. He followed the sickening crunching, and then a pair of eyes reflected the silver of the moonlight as they moved towards him. He stepped back and loosed the shot with a snap of his wrist. There was a solid crack followed by a short snarl, and then there was something moving in from his right-hand side, the grass rustling in its wake. He dropped the sling and managed to pull the short knife from his belt before the wolf tore his throat out.

Barra picked up a lance and tested the sharpened point before taking up his stance. He glanced across at Ide, winked and then turned back to the target: a flat stone with an almost circular hole through the middle strung from the branch of a tree.

Barra pushed strands of flaming red hair from his eyes and looked over at Finan standing between him and the target. 'It's too close,' he complained, 'I can't get a proper throw at it.'

The smaller, darker man laughed. 'And what will you do if the Fomor come riding south one of these fine days, eh? Ask them to wait while you work out the range?'

Barra laughed, and then, drawing back his arm, loosed the spear. The slim javelin flew high and its underside scraped along the upper edge of the stone.

Barra swore and, in one smooth movement, pulled up

another javelin from the ground and threw. The polished length of wood went neatly through the centre of the hole.

Ide laughed and clapped her hands, and Barra, glancing across at her was momentarily startled, for with the setting sun on her red hair it looked as if it were aflame.

Finan came over to him and handed back the two spears. 'My turn,' he said, flexing one of the spears slightly, testing its balance.

'Of course, if the Fomor come, you'll make sure you have a spear of the proper weight and the correct balance.'

Finan grinned and assumed his throwing stance, one foot behind and at right angles to the other, the weight on his right foot. He drew his arm back, breathing in and out slowly; his muscles tensed...

And then the wolves howled.

Finan looked at Barra and immediately all thoughts of the contest were forgotten. Moving quickly they gathered up the spears, pulled the stone from the branch and threw it in the back of the chariot. Barra hitched up the horses while Finan stood watch, a spear in his hand and another close by his side, its point stuck into the soft earth. Ide too caught something of their urgency and quickly gathered up the combs and pins with which she had been adorning her hair whilst the men contested the game. She too had heard the stories of the past few weeks about the pack of killer wolves that were roaming the district.

It was impossible to tell how many animals were involved, and although some reports said only one, the destruction was so great that more than one animal had to be involved. Entire fields of sheep had been wiped out, the shepherds and their dogs butchered also. Lonely farmhouses had been attacked and the occupants slaughtered, with the livestock then killed or scattered out into the fields to trample the crops.

And there was evidence of wolves everywhere, but with tracks three times larger than even the largest wolfhound in all Erin. Several parties had gone in search of the animal or animals; all but one hadn't returned, and of the last group there were only three survivors – out of more than twenty men and horses and ten large hunting dogs.

And now most of the fields lay untended, the farmers and country folk having pulled in to the local forts, seeking shelter in the shadow of their walls. A messenger had been sent to Tara to beg help from the king, but neither he nor any word had returned. The roads of western Erin were deserted, with only the occasional heavily armed party of horsemen or company of fast-drawn chariots venturing forth.

Finan brought the chariot around in a tight circle and began the long climb up and out of the small sheltered valley. Barra stood by his left side, a spear clenched in both hands, his sharp green eyes reading the ground ahead and to either side of them. Ide stood between the two men, one hand clutching the side of the bucking chariot, the other holding a bundle of spears.

It was generally accepted that the wolf or wolves were not natural, and it was whispered that they were were-creatures. They were possessed at any rate with unnatural strength and cunning, and certainly did not fear man, as most of the wild creatures did.

Finan was sweating heavily by the time they reached the crest of the hill, and he swung the whip out over the horses' heads, snapping them into a gallop. He knew they would not be able to sustain the pace for long, but once they were out of the low scrubland and stunted trees and onto the flat moorland then he could ease up.

The chariot rattled over the rough track, jolting them to either side. Ide clung to Barra now, who stood with splayed legs watching a movement in the bushes behind and to their left. When he was sure the trembling leaves were moving contrary to the wind, he turned and shouted to Finan above the crack of the breeze, 'We're being followed.'

The small dark man nodded and snapped the whip again, urging greater speed from the already tiring animals. The chariot slewed sideways around a sharp downward bend, spraying the bushes on their left-hand side with grit and small stones, sending crows wheeling skywards. Finan grimaced; crows were the creatures of Morrigan and portents of death. But they were now on the level and racing down across a flat wasteland of stone dotted with tiny clumps of scrub and bush. They could see for miles across the lichen-green and heather-purple stones... and there was nothing moving.

Finan began to breathe more easily. 'Maybe it was just...' he began, and then Ide screamed. Three huge wolves had come out from behind the rocks on their left-hand side. They stood at the foot of the slight decline, unmoving, watching the bucking chariot intently. And then as one they moved, cutting away across country, moving diagonally to their left, until they dropped out of sight behind some rocks.

'By the Gods,' Barra swore, 'did you see the size of those animals?'

'They're going to cut us off,' Finan said, pointing with the whip. 'They'll probably be waiting for us where the road narrows.'

'Can we beat them to it?' Barra asked.

'We'll try,' Finan said, beginning to whip up the horses again, calling up the last of their strength for one final mad gallop.

'What are we going to do?' Ide asked quietly, her panic held tightly under control.

Barra looked at Finan and then back to Ide. He smiled with a confidence he did not feel. 'We'll think of something,' he said.


It was said that Cascarach could charm the birds from the trees, and bring even the most maddened boar to his feet.

It was said that Cascarach was elven, half-elven, a god, a demon...

It was said... but then, many things were said about Cascarach – and most of them were true.

That he was elven – or half-elven – there was little doubt. He stood taller than most other men and was unnaturally thin; his features too were thin and pointed, his eyes slanted, and although he was a man into his eight and twentieth year, he wore no beard and the hair on his head hung loose and shining to his shoulders, unbanded and unbraided. And as a harper he was unsurpassed; generations would come and go before Erin saw even a shadow of his like again in the blind harper, Carolan.*

He was Sighted also.

There was about a fingerspan of wine left in the goblet, and Cascarach was drunk enough to wonder idly whether he should drink it or toss it into the dying fire and watch the flickering flames turn blue and green. He gently ran his long delicate forefinger around the rim of the goblet and allowed the images to form in the blood-red liquid. It was an amusement, nothing more: his Sight would read moments of intense emotion and render them into images for him in any available liquid.

The Harper blinked at what he now saw, and sat up straight, nudging the goblet and shattering the image. He swore and activated the spell again and then fought to make sense of the still swirling image. He curbed his impatience while it settled. His frown deepened, and then slowly turned to fear... and then anger...

The three huge wolves had pulled down the horses, leaving

* see Chapter Five.

the smoking carcasses where they had fallen, and attacked the humans. Barra had managed to place a javelin through the side of one of the creatures, but even as he looked one of the other wolves had gripped the shaft of the spear in its huge jaws and pulled it from the other's flesh. The wound had spurted once and then congealed into a solid crust. Finan swung a spear and rapped another beast across the snout with it, jabbing for the eyes. The wolf snapped, its yellowed teeth closing with an audible click as it covered its stinging nose with its forepaws. The three wolves now paced slowly around the felled chariot, darting in, snapping, darting back out again, slowly wearing the humans down.

Seen close up the wolves were huge creatures, standing as tall, if not taller than the fallen horses, their coats long and seemingly metallic, glinting in the rapidly disappearing light. When night fell, so would the humans.

Ide, Finan and Barra stood back to back, spears in their hands, jabbing when the creatures came too close. Their only great fears were night and exhaustion ... and both were rapidly approaching.


Cascarach began drumming his fingers on the table as he watched the three wolves beginning to circle the fallen chariot and take up positions around it; their next move, he knew, would be to attack simultaneously at the weak link, and the weak link was the woman. He shifted his Sight and, sure enough, the largest of the wolves was now opposite her. He saw the animal's muscles begin to quiver, saw it prepare to jump...


The sheet of lightning ripped open the sky almost above their heads. Ide screamed and stumbled back against the two men, who also staggered with fright. But the three wolves, instead of attacking, also leapt backwards, the whites of their eyes showing. Again and again the lightning tore across the sky, turning the gloom into the brightest semblance of day, etching abstract images into their minds and eyes: *a bush … a tilted stone … the harness of the dead horses … the blood burned black in the light …*

And then a series of forked lightning came to ground around them, pounding the earth with its force, befouling the air with a sharp bitter stench that caught at the throat and eyes. A bush exploded into flames, and a wolf, its coat singed, darted yelping into the night, followed by the second and then the third as a patch of earth was gouged out and a stone shattered with the force of the levin bolts.

Cascarach slumped back exhausted and drained the remainder of the wine in one swallow.

The Harper made his way westwards the following day. His journey took him through the heart of Erin, into the ancient spreading forests and the broad fertile grasslands and out into the rocky wasteland that was Connaught. It wasn't entirely barren – it just seemed that way. But compared with the rest of the island it looked like a cursed place, and indeed, in a future that would have been unimaginable to the Harper and the people of his day, the invader that history would call Cromwell would banish the Irish to Hell or to Connaught, there being little to choose between the two.

But it had its own natural beauty that appealed to the Harper's non-human blood, and he found it stirring feelings inside him that had lain dormant for a long time. Cascarach made his way to the fort of Calte, the local lord, and inquired after the two men and the woman who had recently escaped the wolves. Barra, Finan and Ide were brought before the tall stranger, who told them, in his high, almost musical voice, of the attack of the wolves and the intervention of the lightning.

'How do you know all this?' Barra had demanded, and in reply the Harper had gestured and tiny threads of flame had danced along the warrior's wristlets and down his sword sheath. 'How do I know? Why, because I sent the lightning.'

'Then you know of these creatures?' Calte intervened. He was an old man now, but he had once held his place as one of the foremost warriors in all Erin. 'And if you know of them, what are they ... and more to the point, can you rid us of them?' He sat back against the wall in the large gloomy room, the firelight highlighting the wrinkles in his face, and especially the new ones around his eyes and mouth that had formed in the past few weeks since the wolves arrived.

Cascarach smiled, his teeth unnaturally long and somewhat pointed in the light. 'I made ... enquiries along the way,' he said quietly. 'The wolves are, in fact, the three daughters of the Lord of the White Fort ...' He gestured vaguely to the west. 'You will find no reference to this lord, his lineage or his domain; his title and name were struck from the records and the bards foresworn even to mention his name again.'

'Why?' Finan wondered.

Cascarach smiled and shook his head. 'That, even I do not know. But to continue: these are evil creatures, and they were bound in the form of wolves on account of their crimes generations ago in the Dawn of Man. But it now seems as if they have found some way to break free of their bondage and hunt abroad.'

'But can they be stopped?' Calte demanded.

Cascarach nodded, his pale gold hair shimmering like silk. 'They can ... but it is not easy. And, since the three women were born of the one birth, they must be slain together, with one blow.'

'One blow?'

'One blow!'

Calte smiled in the darkness, one half of his face moving, the other side lost in the shadows. 'If you can bring these three creatures together,' he said softly, 'then I can slay them for you.'

Cascarach nodded. 'Well said, but how?'

'In my youth,' the old lord said, 'I found a spear on the beach just below,' he jerked his thumb back over his shoulder. 'It was longer than any spear I'd ever had, and so I kept and used it.' He paused and sipped from a heavy earthen goblet, and then indicated that Barra and Finan could sit. They squatted down beside the fire whilst Ide remained standing, her hand on Barra's shoulder, her fingers idly toying with a lock of his fire-bronzed hair.

'There were still Fomor abroad in those days,' Calte continued, 'and they would occasionally raid us – and we them. And it was then that I discovered a curious thing about my spear: it never struck just one person, but always two or three, and on one memorable occasion, three warriors and two mounts.' The old man shook his head in fond remembrance and drank again. 'And I remember a time when I went hunting. There was a huge serpent in one of the lakes up north. It had killed many people and destroyed crops and so we – my brothers and I – set out to destroy it. Well my brothers tried, and two of them died attempting it, but when I loosed my spear it struck the creature beneath the mouth, passed through it and continued on through four of the serpent's coils before ending up in its barbed tail. Aye,' he nodded decisively, 'if you can bring the wolves together, I can get the three of them at once for you.'

Bres leaped from the currach and hauled it up the beach, sand scraping along its bottom, but the hide covering, although flexible, was tough. The old man pulled the craft above the high-water mark and then, taking a long reed-woven pot from the wood and hide boat, set off down the beach collecting the finer pieces of sea wreckage. There had been a high tide the previous night and the higher reaches of the beach were strewn with weed and curiously shaped pieces of wood. The old man wandered about the base of the cliffs, slowly and carefully filling the basket strung to his back. Seabirds mewled on the cliffs above his head where they had their nests, and he reflected that if he were ten years younger and if his bones hadn't started to stiffen, he would be up those cliffs in an instant and lifting himself a few eggs. The old man shook his head sadly and stepped back, still looking up, but the nests were well back on a ledge and invisible from the ground. Bres was about to move off when he caught sight of something glinting in the cool mid morning air, something long and fine and metallic. It was probably just a stone, but the more the old man looked at it, the more he was convinced that it was a piece of metal or cloth. He pulled his sling from his belt and looked around for a suitable stone; he had a score or more of almost smooth round stones in the pouch on the left-hand side of his belt, but it would be wasteful to use them...

The first stone struck below the gleaming strand and clattered back down onto the beach. The second was high, but it loosened a small pile of grit and stones which succeeded in sweeping the metallic strand down onto the beach. Bres stooped painfully and brushed aside the grit to pull out the strands. There were about six of them, entwined together; they looked like hair, but felt like bronze...

The old man felt his heart begin to pound painfully as he carefully folded the metallic strands and slipped them into his pouch. Moving as quietly as possible he pulled the basket onto his shoulder and stepped down the beach, sticking to the sandy patches, avoiding the stones. He gently eased the basket into the currach and then began to push it down the beach, wincing as the scraping of sand along its bottom seemed hideously loud on the morning air. As he pushed it into the waves with a sigh of relief, he turned back and looked up the beach towards the cliffs, and from where he stood he could just make out the irregular opening of a cave high on the cliff-face.

At first the notes were inaudible, but they swelled with the sunrise, until it seemed as if the delicate music was part of the dawning of the day. Cascarach the Harper sat crosslegged on a broad flat stone above the cliffs, his head bent, seemingly lost in thought, strumming his whitewood harp absently.

It was two days since Bres had brought the metallic hair to Calte's fort. The lord had immediately mounted an expedition to the sheltered bay, but of the twenty men who had set out, only two survived to tell the tale of the three huge wolves that had attacked them in a long defile that led out onto the beach, slaughtering the men and mounts.

So now Cascarach sat alone; if the wolves came, he would attempt to lull them with his music, subtly suggesting that they might appreciate it more fully if they assumed their human forms.

The Harper played long into the morning, and the sun rode through the heavens, lengthening and then gradually shortening the shadows along the ground, and then slowly beginning to lengthen them again as the afternoon wore on. But the music flowed tirelessly, ceaselessly, testament to Cascarach's inhuman strength and endurance. And then, just as the sun was beginning to dip below the lip of the cliffs and into the chill western ocean, the wolves came. One moment there was nothing, and then the grasses parted, and the three huge creatures were standing before and on either side of him. Cascarach made no sign that he had noticed their presence but merely continued playing, his fingers barely seeming to move, and yet drawing the full power from the ancient instrument.

And the wolves slowly approached, their jaws wide and slavering.

The Harper played then as he had never played before, his music weaving a spell, lulling, soothing and calming the beasts. He knew that if they attacked now, he would have no chance; he could not play and draw upon his other magical powers at the same time. And so he played for his life.

And one by one the great wolves sat down before the solitary figure in the lonely landscape and listened to him play.

Cascarach played long into the night. The stars rose and danced sedately across the heavens before sinking again, and the sky to the east brightened greyly in the false dawn, but still the Harper played. And then, as the first tentative rays of a copper sun sent his shadow wavering long into the dew-damp grass, he stopped.

The wolves' heads came up and their eyes snapped open. 'I need rest, but I will play again this evening,' he said softly. He carefully wiped down his instrument and slipped it back into its ornate case. He stood slowly and massaged the small of his back. 'It is true that dogs – and especially wolves,' he added hastily, 'have a far greater range of hearing than man, but man's hearing is far more subtle.' He smiled. 'And it is impossible to appreciate the full depth and beauty of my music in your present form.' He nodded briefly and, turning his back on the savage animals, walked away from them.


The Harper slept through the day, but by evening, rested and refreshed, he was back on the broad flat stone, his harp on his knee, and this time Calte was lying flat in the long grass off to his left-hand side. They both knew it was a gamble; if the wolves came that way neither Calte nor Cascarach would stand a chance.

The sky in the west came alive with fire-streaked wisps of

cloud against which the tiny black specks of seabirds wheeled and circled. The Harper sat facing the sunset so that the sunrise would be on his back, and then he eased his harp from its case and began to play.

The melody was different this time, it was softer, slower, soothing. It seemed to take on the mood of the evening and magnify it, intensify it – until it seemed as if the very night itself took voice and sang. The birds themselves, saluting the close of the day with a bright flurry of song, grew silent and listened, and soon the trees and bushes around the Harper were bright with tiny burning eyes as the night creatures gathered.

The Harper played into the night allowing nature to dictate his music, weaving the whisper of the grasses and the muttering of the trees into it. The night absorbed his music, enfolding it within its darkness, taking it to itself, becoming part of it.

Suddenly all the fire-bright eyes blinked out and were gone, and the three wolves stood before the Harper. He nodded a greeting and continued playing, but said softly, 'If you were to assume your human forms you would appreciate my music better.'

The wolves took no notice but merely continued staring at the Harper. Cascarach continued playing and the night rode on for midnight, and slowly he began to lower the tone of his nightsong, dropping it down and down until even Calte lying stiff and prone in the wet grass could barely hear it.

There was a sudden movement and the chill air about the wolves shimmered and then something like a skin fell away and the three daughters of the Lord of the White Fort were revealed. They must have been beautiful once, for they still retained a shadow of their former loveliness. That they were of the same stock as the Harper was plain: the high cheekbones, the slanted eyes and pointed chin indicated that, but where they differed was in their eyes. Whereas the

Harper's were bright and alive, the women's were lifeless, resembling large flat stones, seemingly without pupil or white, and their faces were totally devoid of expression.

They swayed in time to the now quickening music, and Calte too could feel its lure; it pulled them in, drawing them closer to the Harper, bringing them together ... and slowly Cascarach bound them in chains of music and held them through the night.

The sky brightened, its greyness spilling across the eastern sky like turgid water, and then out from the greyness light the colour of freshly spilled blood tinged the sky, and the sun rose in the east.

The three women cringed in the bright light; creatures of darkness, twilight or cloudy days, the harsh light of day was painful to them. They attempted to pull away from Cascarach and reach the discarded wolf pelts, but the spell still held. And then as one they turned and lunged for him, their hands clawed, their long nails ready to rend and tear ... and Calte pushed himself to his feet and threw his spear before collapsing back onto the ground.

The weapon hummed as it spun through the air, the pyramidal head revolving rapidly. The razor sharp point struck the nearest woman just above the right breast, passed partially through her body, struck through her sister's chest, and lodged itself in the third woman's throat, locking them together like three gaffed fish. The bodies swayed on their feet, the same expression now irrevocably etched on their faces, and then slowly they began to crumple. The feet went first, turning to a grey and bone-white dust that quickly ate its way up their legs and consumed their bodies, until soon the spear was lying in a pile of dust on the blackened earth.

Cascarach, his harp tucked under one arm, helped Calte to his feet. The old man groaned aloud with the agony of returning circulation and he was shivering with the chill. He limped across to the three mingled piles of dust and nudged them with his foot. 'And that is it?' he asked quietly.

'The werewolves are gone?'

Cascarach nodded and looked out across the sea. 'You know,' he said softly, 'it is the end of an era; for generations creatures like these, werewolves, ghouls, serpents, *peisti*, blood-suckers have come out of the Cave of Crucha.' He looked down at the pile of dust by his feet which was already beginning to be scattered on the wind. 'These were the last of the Dolours Company, the outcasts of this world, banished by the gods and the Tuatha De Danann into the Shadowland. We will not see their like again.'

'Thank the gods for that then,' Calte said, and then looked curiously at the Harper. 'You sound almost sorrowful.'

'I can see my own race going the way they went; shunned, feared, hunted.' He shook his head and walked away from the old lord, taking the path that led down to the beach. 'And each day,' he said quietly, but clearly, 'a little more magic goes from this world.'

# Chapter Four

# THE NINE

The diver emerged spluttering from the icy waves. He hawked, spat a mouthful of salt water and shouted up at the vessel rocking beside him. 'There's no reef, no weed ...' He coughed as a wave slapped across his mouth, and then reached up as the captain leaned over the edge of the low craft and stretched down his arm. Cathal hauled the young man in easily and then called for a blanket. 'There's nothing but clear water as far down as I can see,' the diver continued through chattering teeth.

Cathal nodded his thanks and then turned to the young man in the long white robes of the priests standing beside him. 'Well, what do you think?'

Sesnan shrugged. 'If there is no weed and no reefs – and I don't see how there could be,' he added, indicating the flat expanse of grey water with the smudge of the Pictish coastline to the south and east, 'then the only conclusion I can come to is that we have been trapped by magic.'

The young king nodded. 'It's what I feared. There's not that many reasons for a boat to stop in mid sea without any cause, is there?' he added with a smile. He looked across at the druid, not many years older than himself. 'What would you recommend?'

Sesnan smiled and shrugged again, the bones of his shoulders showing through the thin woollen robe. 'An enchantment of this sort is very localised, and we must therefore assume that whatever is holding us is directly below. Someone will have to go down . . . oh, I can give them some protection,' he added hastily, seeing the look of shock on the king's face.

'I'll go,' Cathal said quickly, recovering from the shock of discovering that someone – or something – beneath the waves was holding them motionless.

'*No!*' The druid's normally calm voice had risen slightly, and he was suddenly conscious that the crew of the becalmed craft were looking at him curiously. 'No,' he repeated in a lower tone, 'you cannot.' He held up his hand to forestall the king's protests. 'I know I said I could give you some protection, but look . . . look all around you; what do you see?'

'Water; Pictland to the south . . .'

The druid nodded, wisps of his thinning white hair falling over his intense eyes. He was an Outlander, a foreigner from the lands far to the east of Banba, beyond the dividing waters, from distant Gaul, and he looked conspicuously out of place amongst the swarthier, smaller Gaels, his blond hair and blue eyes contrasting sharply with the brighter, reddish-bronze, gold or black hair, and the green, black or brown eyes of the islanders. But they respected him because of his Faith and because of his powers, and at four-and-twenty he was one of the youngest men ever to have risen so high in the strict hierarchy of the druids.

He touched the king's arm and led him away from the listening ears of the bewildered and frightened crew. They had set out four days ago to negotiate a treaty with the flaxen-haired northerners, who had recently taken to raiding the coastal towns. Cathal had decided to take three boatloads of men with him, more as a show of strength than as a measure of protection. They had set out along the north-western coast of Banba heading northwards, hugging the relatively sheltered coastal waters – but with the broad Western Ocean beating in incessantly there was little enough shelter anywhere on that bleak coast. Having rounded the tip of Banba they then crossed the icy stretch of water that separated the island from its nearest neighbour. They continued northwards, weaving in and through the countless tiny islands of Pictland and avoiding the many tempting sheltered bays and inlets; many an unwary ship had come to grief in those sheltered inlets at the hands of the barbaric Picts.

That morning they had rounded the tip of Pictland and, although the water was still chill and speckled with tiny clumps of ice, the day was bright and warm – but the wind from the north and west was razor sharp.

And then they had suddenly stopped.

The three craft, moving in a roughly triangular formation, had abruptly ground to a halt as if they had struck a reef, tumbling men to the decks, flinging some into the icy waters. The sails billowed and flapped in the wind, and the waves washed over the sides of the crafts, but they remained unmoving.

Cathal sent teams of divers down, but one by one they had all returned with the same report: nothing, there was nothing down there, no weed, no reefs ...

Which left ... sorcery!


Cathal and Sesnan stood near the bow of the ship, staring down into the dark, grey-green waters. The king's smooth unbearded face was set in grim determined lines, and he had that same set to his mouth that his father had when he had made up his mind about something – and would not be budged.

'Now, why can I not go down?' he demanded. 'You said you could give me some protection.'

'And as I said to you, what do you see all around you?'

'Water!'

'Yes,' Sesnan nodded, 'water ... and I am a druid. I work

with the soil, with growth and life and green things. I draw my magic, my power, from the earth itself. Water is not my element. Here, my powers are weakened and diminished. If I give you protection I cannot guarantee that I can keep it.' He smiled briefly. 'And I will not allow you to risk your life.'

The young king smiled. 'I know that – and I thank you for it. But I must go down; I cannot afford to send anyone else down ... the gods alone know what they might find. In any case, if we have been stopped by some magical power I hardly think it likely that whomever – or *whatever* – has stopped us will allow me to drown. If they wanted me dead and they possess this power they could just as easily have struck me with a thunderbolt or swept me overboard with a gust of wind.'

The druid shook his head and sighed. 'You have the glib tongue of a poet or bard,' he said.


He didn't feel the cold: his limbs were still tingling from the unguent Sesnan had rubbed into them, and although no light seeped in through the grey water he found he could see – not well, but enough to make out vague shapes in the water. He fell, quickly at first, but then more slowly, sinking into the depths of the grim Northern Sea. He kept his arms pressed to his sides and his feet together, his body rigid, allowing the currents to carry him. When the light above him went he twisted his head and, remembering to keep his mouth tightly shut and ensuring that the plugs remained in his nostrils, looked upwards. But the oblong shadows of the ships were gone, and he could see nothing but the blurry twisting of some sea creature against the shifting grey-black waters.

Something darted close to his face and his head snapped back. The urge to cry out was almost overwhelming, and then he saw it was just a tiny shoal of minute fish moving together as one. He found it difficult not to breathe through his mouth and he had to constantly fight against the impulse. He could hear his heart pounding in his head and the druid's last words pounding along with them. 'You are now, in effect, breathing through your skin; the salve will allow it to filter and extract the breath of life. But if you open your mouth the water will destroy you, crushing your lungs, destroying your brain.'

But it was a far easier thing to say than to do when it went against the habit of a lifetime, Cathal decided ironically.

Cathal drifted downwards, whilst all around him the life of this chill sea swarmed. Shoals of fish he vaguely recognised twisted and moved together like a single organism to follow his progress, and other, more recognisable fish, but the size of which he had never imagined, observed him through eyes that seemed alive and alert – and intelligent. Yet other, more sinister creatures coiled smoothly past him, neither fish nor serpent, but something of both. Hideously monstrous sea creatures came forth from the long trailing lengths of weed that now rose from the blackness below him. He must be nearing the bottom. And then he suddenly realised there was nothing below him. His sorcery-enhanced sight enabled him to pierce the utter night of the sea and bring it to a ghastly semblance of daylight, but strain as he might he could see nothing.

The young king loosened his sword in his sheath, the only piece of clothing he wore, and prepared to meet whatever had trapped his ships. His ghost-sight blurred and then something sparkled brightly once and disappeared. For the first time since he had entered the water – how long ago had that been? – he felt cold... an intense and paradoxically burning cold. Sensation disappeared from his hands and feet almost immediately, and then slowly and painfully claimed his arms and legs. He fell into blackness and he knew his sight had gone then, and next his hearing, until the only sound in his universe was the frail beating of his own heart – and even that was slowing.

He was dying.

Perhaps he drifted into unconsciousness or perhaps he continued to fall through the blackness – in the absolute darkness it was impossible to tell, but suddenly there was light: harsh, blinding, painful – and warm – light. He was conscious that he was still and unmoving with something solid beneath his back. Carefully he explored his senses; feeling had returned, and it had been the agonising tingle of returning circulation which had brought him alert. Cathal gritted his teeth and tried not to cry out with the pain ... but he welcomed it also, for it meant he was alive and feeling. And he was sure the dead did not feel.

He was sure he could see: the orange and speckled blackness of his own eyes was clearly visible through his closed eyelids, and he could hear a low sibilant whisper, much as the wind makes through long grass.

Something warm and gentle touched his bare leg and the shock made him sit up suddenly, clutching for his sword – but that was gone, and the sudden effort sent waves of blackness washing over him, and his first – and last – image was of a startlingly beautiful young woman before he lapsed into unconsciousness.

When he awoke again it was night – or what passed for night in this strange kingdom. Although the sky was clear there were no stars strewn across the heavens and no moon rode the skies like some great bird; instead, long trailing wisps of speckled white light drifted lazily overhead like strewn gauze, and although it lacked the hard brilliant beauty of the night stars it had a beauty peculiar to itself.

'It is very beautiful, is it not?' The voice came from behind and Cathal, who had been leaning up on one elbow to stare at the sky, started and swivelled around to face the voice. It belonged to the young woman he had seen briefly before passing out. At first sight she seemed very small, but in effect she was nearly as tall as the young king. She was very beautiful – that was the first fact that impressed itself upon him, and she possessed a strangely exotic beauty. But, by the same token, her looks were not of faerie: her features lacked the angularity of the elven folk, and her breasts – for she was naked – were full and large nippled, unlike the *mna-shee* who were always small breasted like children. Her eyes were large and round, slightly protruding he discovered later, and seemed to blink very slowly and deliberately. Her nose was small, slightly tilted, her lips thin and she spoke through a tiny gap in her mouth, without moving her lips or showing her teeth. Her neck was perhaps longer than the women of Banba, and although her breasts were full, her waist was incredibly slim, and her thighs and legs ended in the tiniest feet Cathal had ever seen.

She smiled, again without opening her mouth, and spoke in a lilting accent. 'You are Cathal, son of a king and king in your own right of the westernmost province of Banba.' It was a statement rather than a question.

The young man came slowly to his feet, wincing as his stiffened muscles protested. 'I am; and who are you?'

'I am Samde,' the young woman said quietly. She walked past him and began to make her way down through a field of tall grass. Cathal lurched to his feet and staggered after her. He looked back over his shoulder and found he had been lying on a small flat-topped knoll that rose from the field like a great basking whale.

Samde cut diagonally through the waist-high emerald-green grass, making for a stand of stunted trees that clustered at one side of the field. As the young king neared them he could see that they resembled stunted, incredibly old oaks, and time had etched human-like masks into the gnarled trunks. The branches – the topmost of which was no higher than his head – began to rustle and quiver as he followed the young woman through the trees, and soon the entire copse was trembling as if in a stiff breeze. The rustling branches cast shadows on the trunks below, and the twisted faces twitched and gibbered with a shadow-life. But Samde strode unafraid through the trees, occasionally brushing one aside with the flat of her hand if it came too close to the track, and where she touched it the wood darkened and scorched. She led the young king out from the copse and into another field. It was smaller than the first, and made even more so by the large circle of standing stones that dominated the centre of the field.

The stones were taller than the king, fashioned of a smooth green stone through which white and silver veins ran like wrinkles. Cathal counted seven and twenty of them standing in a perfect circle. And before every third opening sat a young woman. As he neared Cathal thought they were Samde's sisters, but as he entered the circle and looked around he realised that they were identical to her. He turned slowly, looking at each of the nine in turn – and as he completed a full circle he discovered that Samde had disappeared and he couldn't pick her out from the other women.

The nine women regarded him coldly, their eyes sharp and appraising, and Cathal began to grow uncomfortable beneath their direct gaze. 'What do you want?' he demanded, fear and anger raising his voice to a shout. 'By what right do you hold my ships in thrall?'

'Right? We recognise no right.' The voice, identical to Samde's, came from his right.

'We heed no rights,' a second voice added from behind him.

'Save our own.' And this from off to his left.

Cathal spun around to face each woman in turn. It was like looking at nine polished shields, each one reflecting the same warrior. He stopped and held his pounding head in his hands and concentrated on breathing evenly and deeply. When he looked up the fear and anger were gone from his eyes and his voice was calm. He faced the woman directly across from him. 'Why have you stopped my ships?' he asked quietly.

The woman nodded and a smile touched her thin lips. 'Because we want you,' she said simply.

'Me?' He laughed. 'You will get little ransom for me.'

The woman smiled, the corners of her mouth twisting upwards without showing her teeth. 'What use would we have for your baubles?' She shook her head. 'No, king, it is you we want.'

'What for?' Cathal demanded angrily, attempting to quell the rising fear that threatened to send him grovelling to the ground.

'You will perform a single service for each one of us,' she continued in the same flat monotone. 'If, at the end of nine nights, that service has been completed successfully, then you and your ships are free to leave.'

Cathal nodded grimly. 'And what is this service?'

'You will lie with each one of us for one night,' she said quietly, 'and if on the morning of the tenth day one – just one – of us has conceived, then you may go.'


It was physically and mentally impossible to tell the women apart; they looked identical, felt the same and even reacted the same way. It was as if they were copies or parts of the same person. None of the women seemed to take any pleasure from the physical act, and they regarded it as a necessary duty.

However, over the next nine nights Cathal did piece together enough to recreate part of the women's history.

They were the children – the spawn – of Sinde, the sorceress who had come to the island in the dawn of the world with the princess Caesir Banba, fleeing the rising floodwaters in the east. Then the plague had come and decimated the princess' followers, and Sinde alone survived

– but briefly. She had fallen or jumped – accounts differed – into the sea from a cliff, and had been dashed to pieces on the rocks below – nine distinct pieces in fact. And the magic and power which had been part of her life now followed her into death. Her body regenerated, and the nine parts assumed the original's shape, appearance, memories and abilities... but the emotions, which were part of the soul, were lost with the sorceress' death.

And the Nine were one and yet individual, and their powers – either singly or as a unit – were incredible. For generations they had worked beneath the waves creating a timeless pocket of magic-spawned land, imbuing it with what they imagined, or remembered, of the world above. But it was a precious illusion – and the nine knew it. And knew also that they were weakening and the illusion was dying.

The magic was fading from the world of men, and its effects were slowly seeping through into the depths of the ocean, gradually eroding the pocket of timelessness of its vitality, and beginning to touch the women with age. They realised then that they needed new life if they were to survive; they would have to bring forth children... children in their own image.

And Cathal had been chosen to be the father of this new generation.

And the children, being born of the sea and surrounded by it, would be able to draw their magic and strength from the ceaseless waves.

And having a human sire would allow them to cull the vitality of the land... and they would rule the land and the seas.

The Nine had first constructed a series of Gates through which they could look out onto the world of man. Generations passed while they scanned the times and places of the world alien to them, seeking the one who would be the father of their children. They had watched the launch of the three craft from the west coast of Banba and followed its progress carefully. Something about them attracted the Nine, and they had eventually narrowed it down to two people: Cathal and Sesnan the Druid, but they had chosen the king over the druid for his looks, youth and royal blood.

The nights passed slowly for the king, and what had at first seemed a novelty soon grew boring and then agonising. The women were completely unresponsive and were loath to even touch him, and yet were always extremely careful and gentle. They never kissed.

Eventually the nine nights passed and in the cool light of morning Cathal once again stood in the centre of the stone-enclosed circle and waited as the women passed judgement upon themselves. And one by one they slowly shook their heads and said quietly, 'I have not conceived . . .' until all but one, the women directly before Cathal, had spoken.

The king stared at her desperately, his eyes sunken and feverish. 'And you,' he demanded harshly, 'have you conceived?'

For a long moment there was silence, and then the corners of her mouth twitched and turned up, and for the first time since he had encountered the Nine Cathal saw something like life sparkle in their eyes. She nodded once. 'Yes, I have conceived.'


When Cathal awoke he was lying on his back on the rough boards of his ship staring up into the concerned face of Sesnan the Druid. 'We thought you drowned,' he said simply.

The druid helped the king into a sitting position, and Cathal clung to him and squeezed his eyes shut as the world spun around him and black spots sparked before his eyes. 'Where are we . . .?' he whispered, his voice raw and hoarse.

111

'Still in the same position... we haven't moved.'

'But... but how did you maintain the position for so long?' he croaked.

Sesnan looked puzzled. 'You have been gone barely an hour,' he said quietly, and then he nodded in understanding. 'Aaah, but you forget that time in the Shadowlands marches to a different beat than in our own world. How long were you gone?'

'Nine days,' the king whispered in wonder.

'And but an hour has passed here,' Sesnan said, helping the king to his feet and holding him while he found his legs.

Cathal braced himself and waited until the druid dropped his supporting hand. He breathed deeply, savouring the fresh salt air. 'Give the order,' he said loudly, 'we are free to go.'


Cathal's mission to the east was not successful; captured and imprisoned upon landing, he and Sesnan spent several years in captivity while the rest of his crew were sold into slavery. However, after several desperate bids for freedom, they eventually escaped with the aid of the druid's magic and the king's wits. They freed a score or more slaves who in turn liberated more and then, with a captured ship, they set out for Banba.

They came south this time, avoiding the spot where they had been captured and held the last time, and sailed around the coast of the Britons, over the spires of sunken Lyonesse, and then swung north again, passing Mona, but now keeping the coast of Banba in sight at all times on their port side. Some of the crew of freed slaves had been part of Cathal's original crew, and they wept openly at the sight of their homeland. It had been seven years – almost to the day – since they had first set out from the wild western shores of the island. It felt good to be coming home.

★

The morning was like a flawless gem; crystal clear and bright, with even the most distant landmarks and islands clearly visible. No clouds marred the heavens and there was little or no breeze.

Cathal and Sesnan stood in the prow of their stolen craft just behind the carven figurehead and watched the coast of Banba rise up from the sea. Behind them the men rowed strongly, a low rumbling sea-shanty helping to maintain the beat; for some it was a homecoming, for others a chance to start again as free men.

The years spent in captivity had changed both men; Cathal had lost the boyish flesh of his youth and had hardened into a warrior. His flesh had tanned and darkened and although not yet thirty summers his reddish hair was now flecked with silver. And the only remaining vestige of his youth was the occasionally innocent look in his eyes.

Time had dealt a little more harshly with the druid. He had never been fleshy but he was now thin, his hair gone except for tufts above his ears, giving his face a skull-like appearance. His intense eyes had sunk deep into his face, like coals burning through cloth, and his pale complexion had turned sallow. But his power was undiminished.

Sesnan looked up suddenly, his head tilted back, his nose questing like a hunting dog's. He moved his head from side to side in an attitude of listening.

'What is it?' Cathal asked.

'Something...'

'What?'

'A ... disturbance; something... something powerful is approaching.'

The metal craft came up from beneath the waves in an explosion of foaming water. The rhythm of the oarsmen was broken and several men were struck by the flailing lengths of wood. Shrieks of fear mingled with the moans of those with broken bones or cracked ribs, and as the craft lost momentum it began to wallow in the flat sea.

The strange craft bobbed on the waves nearly two lengths away from them. It was a small arrow-shaped vessel, high both fore and aft, and with a single mast set amidships. It was constructed – or perhaps sheathed – of metal, a shade something between copper and gold. In the early morning sunshine it was afire with reflected light, and the figures moving about the deck were little more than shadows.

The metallic craft began to move towards them, drifting contrary to the waves. It turned out of the light, the fire died, and the figures on the deck leapt into stark relief. And although they were dressed in long flowing black robes, Cathal immediately recognised them as the Nine.

The strange craft edged closer, until it was barely a length away from the ship. The women lined the rail: nine identical, motionless figures in black, only the ovals of their faces visible, their eyes startlingly bright. There was a sudden shifting movement and the woman nearest Cathal held up a small black-swathed bundle. 'Behold your son,' she called, her voice echoing slightly across the waves, and then she twitched the cloth aside. In her strong, bone-white hands she held a young boy high out over the water. The resemblance between him and the king was unmistakable: the same startling red hair, the same high bone structure and jutting jaw. But he also carried the other-worldly strangeness of his mother, the same flat expressionless eyes, the same tight-lipped grimace. The child reached out with long-fingered groping hands.

'My son?' Cathal whispered.

'No,' the druid said quietly, 'the seed may have been yours, but the womb that carried it and the woman that bore it are not human; there is nothing of you in that child.'

'My son...' The king stared entranced at the child. To return to Banba with a boy-child – a son – would make up for all those missing years. A son, and something his father, Ridonn, King of Munster would appreciate. He looked across at the child again; handsome aye, and well formed.

He would grow up to be a fine young man. A son any father might be proud of. Impulsively he reached across for the child.

Sesnan struck down his outstretched hands. 'It is not your child,' he insisted fiercely. 'Take it and you are taking your own destruction, aye, and the destruction of Banba unto yourself. That... that child has more power than the greatest druids ever dreamed of. The child is master of the sea! Take it, accept it, invite it into your fort and remember, by inviting evil in you grant it leave to work. You will enable it to consolidate its power with the magic of the soil and stones. In effect you will have enabled it to become the most powerful creature in this world, both on land and sea...' The druid trailed off, realising the king was not listening to him. He was clearly entranced.

Cathal looked across at the young boy, still dangling from his mother's hands. His son.

*'Father... take me... I am yours... take me...'*

Cathal ignored the tiny voice whispering insistently inside his head and looked up at the mother. 'How is he called?' he asked.

*'NO!'* Sesnan shouted, drowning out her reply. He grabbed Cathal's arms and swung him around. He stared deep into his eyes... and drew back suddenly, for there was no recognition there. 'Do not ask his name,' the druid said forcefully, 'do not take any part of him to yourself.'

The king pushed the older man aside almost casually, sending him sprawling to the deck, leaving him there while he turned back to the woman and repeated his question.

'He is unnamed; his naming is yours, he is your son.'

*'I am your son... take me... take me...'*

The druid pushed himself to a sitting position and threw up his hands, calling down his magic. A huge wave rose up between the two ships and crashed down on the metallic craft, sending it spinning away from them. And now a wind began to blow from the south and west, filling the huge cloth sail, sending it cracking taut on the mast. The longship leaped forward, tumbling many of the unprepared crew to the decks. Cathal fell beside the druid and when he looked up there was murder in his eyes. Sesnan gestured again as the king reached for his knife, and Cathal felt his muscles lock and freeze into rigid bands. The druid held up one long forefinger. 'Trust me and wait,' he said gently.

Now the crew had found their positions and were pulling strongly towards the west, and the craft fairly skimmed across the waves, foaming white-water spraying up on either side. The rocky coastline of Banba quickly solidified and took on both shape and definition, a strip of golden beach highlighting the solid blackness of the jagged cliffs.

But now the metallic craft was turning about, and slowly and inexorably it gained on them.

Sesnan made his way to the prow and continued working his magic. The closer they came to shore the stronger he became ... but he needed something more, and he needed it now. He leaned against the smooth polished wood of the figurehead, his damp palms staining the wood – and then something like a spark leaped from it to his skin. And suddenly he knew. His ancestors, the forebears of the current invaders, had known the magic of imprisoning some of the lesser spirits – usually the spirit or sprite of the material, be it wood, stone or leather, in which they were working. When they constructed a craft such as this they usually imprisoned the elemental in the snarling figure-head, and then, in times of greatest danger, they would call it up, using its raw energy to come to their aid. The current generation didn't know the craft – but they were shipbuilders and they followed the old ways, and perhaps a little of the old magic might yet remain.

The druid stood behind the figurehead and placed both hands flat against the sides. His head tilted back and his eyes rolled shut. He allowed the force to gather within him and then he slowly and reluctantly allowed it to trickle out

116

through his fingers and into the wood. He felt the rush of energy leave him and he felt the cool wood begin to heat up and the wooden side of the snarling figurehead assume a warm fleshy texture. Slowly he ran his hands down the dragon-shape . . . and slowly the ship came alive beneath his hands.

Raw power pulsated through the boards, lifting the craft clear of the waves and the oarsmen were thrown back on their benches, watching stupidly as their oars rattled uselessly in their locks. The cloth sail filled and stretched on the mast until it threatened to burst asunder.

But the vessel of the Nine continued to approach.

And then the boards began to smoulder and burn with the power that now ran through them. Wisps of smoke rose only to be shredded on the wind – but it was the same wind which now fanned the fires. The decks and rails went first, the wood darkening, the grain blackening in abstract patterns, and then, when the decks grew too hot to stand upon, the blackened wood began to flake away in stinging cinders. And then the mast went. There was a sudden explosion as the wood burst into a pillar of flame and almost instantly collapsed, draping the deck with thick sailcloth which immediately began to burn, spreading fire everywhere. The crew worked frantically to toss the burning cloth overboard, but the damage had been done: small fires now dotted the deck, the rowers' benches were burning and even the oars were crisped and blackened.

But the shore was very close now.

The burning sailcloth which had been thrown overboard lay directly in the path of the Nine's vessel, and the metallic hull cut partially through the thick hide before sticking fast, bringing the craft to a lurching halt.

Sesnan slumped against the figurehead exhausted. Perhaps the spell had been incorrectly set, perhaps he had invoked the elemental incorrectly, but the ship should never have burned. He winced as he felt the heat through the thin soles of his boots ... and he suddenly remembered the king: he had left Cathal lying spellbound on the deck ...

The king's leather jerkin and breeches had absorbed much of the heat, but his face, arms and legs were raw and blistered, and there was a look of madness in his eyes.

The bottom of the longship scraped sand, and then ripped along a hidden rock; water boiled and hissed as it splashed over onto the blistering decks. The craft lurched, recovered, and lurched again, rending itself against a sandbar before finally shuddering to a halt. And now with no wind and flying water to dampen the fire, the flames leapt forth while the men threw themselves into the shallow sea, more frightened now of the flames than of the metallic craft closing in fast behind them.

Sesnan helped the king to his feet and, half carrying, half pulling, brought him to the ground. The king could barely stand and was forced to lean against the druid for support. His hand, which had been twisted clawlike by the heat, gripped Sesnan's arm through the soiled white cloth of his robe with painful intensity. Sesnan drew the king from the burning ship and through the shallows to a small crag of rock that rose out from the water just behind the stricken vessel. He made to turn away and return to the ship, but Cathal caught his robe and pulled him back.

'I will have my son,' he gasped, his breath coming hard and fast.

Sesnan shook his head. 'I am truly sorry, my friend; sorry for the injuries I have caused you, and sorry because I cannot allow you to take that child.'

*'Don't listen to him father ... take me ... take me ... I am your son ... your son ...'*

'My son,' Cathal said slowly.

'He is inhuman,' Sesnan insisted.

'My son.'

'No!'

*'Yes!'* And Cathal plunged his dagger into the druid's

chest, driving upwards into the heart. There was an instant before death claimed him in which the druid's eyes registered something more than pain and surprise, something that was perhaps close to fear, and then the light of life died in them and he slumped into his friend's arms. Cathal stepped back and allowed the corpse to slide to the rocks, where the waves were quickly tinged with crimson.

'Your son.'

'*Father...*'

'My son!' Cathal held out his hands for the boy, and the mother lifted him high once as if in offering, before throwing him across the space that separated the metallic craft from the king.

And then there was perhaps a moment, a moment when time itself stood still, and Cathal saw several things at once. He saw the mother smile, saw four tusklike fangs glisten in the light, saw the same light glisten off countless shimmering scales on her skin, saw the child flying through the air arms outstretched, saw himself reaching out, felt the weight in his hands, felt the pain – the agonising, searing pain of his crippled hands – saw the child slipping, saw the robe falling away, saw its body and the interlocking scales and the misshapen feet, saw him strike the blood-stained rock, his head bursting asunder like rotten fruit, heard him scream, saw the tusks again, saw a black forked tongue...

'My son,' Cathal whispered, blackness overwhelming him, sending him tumbling forward into the bloody waves.

## Chapter Five

# THE HARPER

He was a small, round-faced man, his balding head fringed
with tufts of iron-grey hair. His clothes, now shabby and
patched, had once been of good quality and he wore them as
if they still retained their former finery. His only
possessions seemed to be a knobbed walking stick and a
wood and decorated leather harp case. He was blind and
called Carolan ... and the finest harper in all Ireland, if not
the world.

The funeral procession made its way slowly along the
winding country road, the wailing of the women and the
professional keeners mingling with the creaking of the cart
and the dull plodding of the horses' hooves. On the cart a
plain wooden coffin rattled against the boards, the new nails
sparkling in the morning light. A large group of people
followed the cart, led by the deceased's young wife, her
family and the local priest. She was weeping uncontrollably,
damning both god and man in her grief, whilst the
neighbours looked on and whispered amongst themselves,
puzzled at young Ian's sudden and inexplicable death.

The young man – married not eight weeks previously –
had been out in the fields, helping with the haymaking. It
was one of those long hot and dry days that seem to linger
on long after they should, holding a memory of the summer
past. Ian had stripped to the waist and had climbed atop a

hay rick and was tying down a large sheet over the top of the rick when the wind blew up out of nowhere and swept across the field. Warm at first, it had rapidly chilled and intensified almost to gale force; chaff and stubble were lifted and spun through the air, tiny stones hissed and buzzed through the still standing grains, and the grass was flattened in a broad swath as the wind moved across the field in a solid – but contained – mass. Most of the field hands were thrown to the ground and lay there while the wind passed over them... but some were caught in it. With most it was just a case of grit or dust in their eyes, but others were not so lucky. One young man running across the field when the wind struck was caught with one foot in the air. He was spun around with the force of the wind and fell hard on his arm, and the sound of breaking bone was clearly audible above the wind's passing. Another had just placed a ladder up against a rick and had started to climb when it struck. The frail wooden steps were jerked from under him, throwing him headfirst into the rick, lacerating his skin and cracking nearly a dozen ribs.

But for some reason the cold wind seemed to vent its full fury upon the rick on which Ian was standing and, curiously, he was seen to strike out with his pitchfork – which was later found with its head snapped off. The leather sheet was ripped from his grasp, striking him roughly across the chest and shoulders, sending him rearing upwards. He balanced precariously, his arms windmilling... and then the top of the hay rick dissolved beneath his feet, carefully stretched and tied straw flying in all directions. Ian's scream was lost as he fell downwards into the heart of the rick, which was immediately torn asunder by the wind's icy fury.

And when they pulled him out from the remains of the rick he was dead, and with not a mark on his body.


The Harper's blind white eyes blinked and his head turned

in the direction of the wailing. He recognised the sound immediately; the ritual keening for the soul of the recently deceased, mingled with the genuine cries of grief by the relatives and friends. He turned his head slightly, listening. His sensitive hearing caught the steady beat of the horses' hooves, the creak of the harness and the rattle of the iron-shod wheels over the rough ground. Gripping his gnarled walking stick tightly he pulled himself to his feet, facing the direction of the sound. Behind, and above his head, a four-armed signpost shifted slightly in the wind and the dust of the crossroads was whipped up into his face. He turned his face away as grit clogged his nostrils and battered against his useless eyes; there were times, he mused, when having no sight was an advantage: you would never be troubled with grit in your eyes for a start!

He had lost his sight at the age of fourteen from smallpox. It should have killed him – and there had been times when he wished it had – but it had taken his sight and departed, like a thief in the night. There had been times also when he had been tempted to take his own life, but ... and there was always that *but*; the *'but'* that was composed of fear, determination and religion.

And then he had gradually become aware of new sensations and the sensitivity of his other senses: hearing, smell, taste and touch. Especially hearing and touch. He was apprenticed to a harper, and he found a strange fascination for this, the most difficult of instruments, and the speed at which he mastered it was almost frightening. He would often spend hours just tracing over and over again the intricate spiralling design on the smooth polished wood of the soundbox of the harp his teacher had given him, and his rounded fingernails would caress the myriad strings, drawing just a ghost of a sound from them.

When he was twenty-one – and had far surpassed the old teacher – he had set out along the lonely hedge-lined roads, feeling the breath of the wind on his face, hearing the whispered rustling of the leaves and tasting the freshness of the air. He would often spend days in one place, learning from the old harpers, building up his repertoire, creating his own compositions before taking to the road again.

He had been on the road for over a year before he came to the tiny village in the west, in sight of the broad Atlantic and close enough to the sea to hear the hollow booming of the waves against the towering Cliffs of Moher. There was no harper in the village, and the local piper was an old, old man, blind and almost deaf, his fingers stiffened by age and hard work. The old man played occasionally, his fingers moving automatically, for he could no longer hear himself play, and he played only dirges because he was incapable of playing quickly with his crippled hands. There was nothing there for Carolan – and yet he stayed. There was something about the district, something that appealed to him. By day he would wander the roads and tracks about the village, allowing his acute senses to lead and guide him, and invariably he found himself drawn to one particular field where he would sit on the crest of a small hillock and listen to the wind, taste its salt freshness and feel its touch on his blind eyes.

And he would hear the music.

It was faint at first, the merest tendril of brittle sound, but he found that if he lay against the ground the music swelled in volume and took on a fragile clarity. And he would often spend the night there, huddled beneath a thin blanket, listening to the ethereal music – and unable to tell whether it came from the ground or from inside his own head.

And it wasn't until he was leaving the village that the old piper told him that he had been sleeping atop a faerie rath.


'Of your charity, sir, if you would play a dirge for us.' The voice, although young, was tinged with an infinite

123

weariness, as if he had seen so much pain and suffering that nothing more could surprise him.

'You would be the priest?' the Harper asked and looked up, and the priest gasped in surprise at the sightless white ovals. And he knew of only one blind harper...

'You are Turlough Carolan?' he asked quietly.

The Harper nodded silently.

The priest glanced back down the road to where the procession could just be seen rounding the bend, the heads of the people visible over the hedges. He had gone on ahead after the short service in the home of the deceased to prepare the grave. He had been surprised to find the small man standing beneath the signpost, a harp case in his arms, his head bent as if lost in thought.

'What ails you father?' the Harper asked suddenly.

Startled, the priest hesitated before answering. 'What...?'

'I may have lost my sight, but God recompensed me in other ways. You are troubled, that much is obvious. Something worries you; what I wonder?' he mused. 'The funeral... the deceased...? Aye, the deceased,' he nodded decisively. 'And why should you worry about the dead? Perhaps because the death was not natural?' He nodded briefly. 'Not natural, but not murder,' he continued shrewdly, reading more from the priest's silence, the quickened heartbeat and breathing than a sighted man could ever possibly have done. 'So, you are not happy about the death – but it was not murder, and yet it was not natural... there was therefore another agency involved; a supernatural agency perhaps?' He turned his blind eyes up towards the priest. 'How did the death occur, father?'

There was silence for a long time after that, and then the Harper heard a sound that was partway between a sob and a gasp. 'I don't know,' the priest confessed, 'but, God forgive me, I think the faeries took him.'

*

Carolan was standing beside the priest when the funeral procession stopped at the crossroads. The mourners had grown silent and only the broken sobbing of the dead man's wife was audible above the whistling of the wind. The Harper waited until everyone was still and he had their positions fixed in his mind's eye before moving forward. With his every sense alert, he reached out with his long delicate fingers and touched the crude wooden box: there *was* something... His fingers tingled as they did when he brought a new song to life, birthed from the murmurings of the wind and rain. He breathed deeply, inhaling the cold damp air that tugged at his lungs. He tasted it like a liquid, mentally removing the odours of horse, man, raw wood, heather and damp grass... and *yes*, there was a tinge of exotic spices on the air: the tell-tale touch of faerie. Slowly he turned his head from side to side. He cut out the anxious whispers of the people, the impatient stamping of the horse, the creak of the harness; he could hear something, the merest whisper on the wind, the shadow of...? He moved closer to the coffin. Above the corpse a ghost of the elven call still lingered.

The Harper moved back to the priest. He was sweating and there was a flush to his skin. When he spoke his voice trembled slightly. 'Quickly, give me my harp; he is not dead – not yet!'

The priest pressed the heavy leather case into the Harper's hands. Carefully, and with something approaching reverence, the Harper undid the laces and slipped the harp from its case. The morning light ran like liquid along its polished surface, nestled in the runic scrollwork, giving it depth and striking fire from the strings.

The Harper sat down on a milestone by the side of the road, rested his long delicate fingers on the strings and began to play. His fingers moved and yet there was a long moment's silence as if he hadn't touched them. And then it seemed as if the wind itself took voice. It began as a low, barely felt trembling in the air, like the humming of a branch in the wind, and then it grew and swelled, the sound growing, strengthening. Tiny minor notes spun and darted, gone before they could be truly identified, but adding to the music's intensifying spell. The Harper's fingers seemed to barely move and yet the incredibly delicate music grew and took on body, enveloping the silent procession in its spell. It called to them, plucked at some deeply hidden and forgotten part of them; and the mourners felt an incredible longing . . . but for what, they could not say, except that they felt a *loss*.

And then the tenor of the music changed as Carolan called the faerie folk to himself. Although it was still soft and entrancing, it now had a stronger commanding core to it. It compelled, for it was the song of the untameable elements. And it drew the faerie folk.

The mourners could see nothing, hear nothing save the music, and yet they knew with an absolute certainty that the *gentry* had come. The very taste of the air had changed, from fresh and chill to hard and metallic and touched with the flavour of exotic spices. Many felt the tell-tale icy chill along their spines or at the base of their necks, and those who were fey actually saw the sudden thickening of shadows about the Harper and above the coffin.

Carolan looked up from his harp, a tiny smile on his lips. 'Ah, so you came.'

'*You knew we would; you knew we had no choice.*' The voice was like that of a child's, thin, high and pure but, unlike a child's, tinged with absolute weariness. '*What do you want, harper?*'

'The soul of this young man.'

'*We do not have his soul; that belongs to his god.*'

'I want that part of him which you have stolen.'

To the silent watchers it seemed as if the Harper were holding a conversation with the empty air, and yet the horse was terrified, rolling its eyes and trembling all over, too frightened even to run.

'*What is this man to you?*' the voice demanded. '*He is nothing.*'

'He is human... and he has a wife who grieves for a husband lost before his time.' The Harper's fingers brushed the strings and the ethereal music spun out once again. The shadows wavered and solidified slightly, assuming a definite man-like form, although taller and thinner than anyone present.

Carolan smiled. 'At the moment I have only called forth a tiny part of you, but take care lest I call you into the full light of day.'

'*You have not the power,*' the voice stated flatly.

'You forget, creature, that I learned my craft on the barrows of your people. The birds and beasts are mine to control, aye, and even the very elements should I so wish.' The Harper's rich voice rose, taking on a commanding note. 'So have a care lest I drag you forth from your duns and raths and hidden places and let the pure light of the sun shrivel you.'

The shadows about the coffin moved in agitation and slowly began to shred and fragment, like wind-blown smoke. The creature's words drifted back to the Harper as if from a great distance. '*So be it, harper. You may have that part we have of him – but we did not take his heart, he gave that of his own free will, and that will always be ours!*'

There was a sudden scream, followed by the sound of pounding. The lid of the coffin moved and then abruptly splintered and fell off. Ian sat up.

There was a stunned silence, during which the priest and the mourners stared incredulously at the 'corpse'. And then the priest slowly crossed himself and dropped to his knees on the road and began to pray aloud. Slowly the entire funeral procession followed his example.

127

And then Ian began to scream, a long drawn-out soul destroying scream, a scream of terrible loss or absolute insanity. Again and again he screamed like a demon, until the Harper fingered his harp and the young man fell back into the coffin, unconscious.

They carried him back to his own small house where, with the attentions of the local doctor and a drop of whiskey, he regained his senses. When he opened his eyes he looked curiously about the small dark bedroom as if seeing it for the first time, and then he smiled tentatively and reached for his wife's hand. 'Ah Mary... I've had such a terrible dream...'

The young man drifted in and out of unconsciousness for the next few days, and occasionally when he awoke the light of madness burned bright in his eyes. But the Harper was always there, and his music soothed and calmed him. However, in his sleep, he ranted and raved and, coupled with what he told them during his lucid moments, Carolan and Mary were able to piece together his tale.

He had been atop the hay rick tying down the sheet when he had heard the galloping. It sounded as if a troop of well-shod horses were rapidly approaching, which was strange because there were few troops in the district, and certainly none mounted. He had stood on the hay rick and looked about and sure enough, out from the woods to the south – or rather out from *above* the woods to the south – came a troop of mounted... *men?*

They were taller than mortal men and even their steeds seemed unnaturally tall and thin. The riders were dressed in strange shining armour that shimmered and sparkled as if it reflected sunlight – even though the sun was in the wrong position. Long colourful cloaks streamed behind and they carried glittering swords and delicately wrought spears.

The faerie host – for he knew what it was – raced past him, almost six feet above the level of the ground – and yet he could see the sparks struck by the horses' hooves. He felt the wind of their passage as the host rode by, felt it pluck and tug at him, saw the men in the field below falling, buffeted by the wind, saw others cowering, saw the thin, sharp-boned faces of the riders laughing. He was seized by an almost uncontrollable anger: how dare they do this; by what right did they terrify men, and then laugh at their fear? The last man was galloping towards him. Ian pulled the long pitchfork from the hay beside him and faced the creature. He saw the look of surprise on the elven lord's face, and then a cruel smile touched his lips, and beneath his ornate plumed helm his face hardened into a mask of absolute inhumanity. His sword seemed to leap from its scabbard and come alive in his hand, darting, twisting, moving of its own accord. Ian lunged, and the elven warrior easily parried the clumsy blow, and the slightly curved sword sliced through the wooden handle of the fork as if it were no more than butter.

And Ian had one last glimpse of the elven mount's wild yellow eyes before the gleaming length of the sword swung down... and he had awoken after a series of terrifying dreams in a coffin.


Turlough Carolan went his way some days later, convinced that there was nothing more he could do for the young man. Ian McGee was healthy and fit and already showed signs of throwing off the effects of the strange bout of living death he had undergone.

But as the years passed, however, a hint of the old madness returned, and whenever a cold wind blew he would cower in a corner, screaming.

He took to walking the moors calling for them, and he would often race from hilltop to hilltop, trying to catch any vagrant scrap of wind. And it was said that he had left part of his soul behind in the Shadowland, or perhaps he had given his heart to one of the *mna-shee*, and it was well known that once one had been taken by the faeries one was never truly normal again.

On the twenty-fifth of March, 1738, Turlough Carolan died in Aldford, in the country of Roscommon. His funeral and wake was a huge affair, for the Harper, in his travels around Ireland, had made many friends and was much loved. Mary McGee travelled the hundred or so miles to the wake to pay her last respects to the man who had brought her husband back to life. But when she returned her husband was dead. It seemed he had climbed atop a hay rick and stood there as he had once before. Perhaps he lost his balance and fell ... perhaps. He was found with a broken neck at the base of the wind-blown rick.

There had been no wind that day.

# Chapter Six

# FAMINE

The harvest had failed – again. For the second year running the potato crop had been struck with blight, leaving the fields sodden masses of rotting vegetables. The spectre of famine and its companion, Death, stalked the land. Entire families were wiped out as sickness and disease decimated the weakened people. Many attempted to flee, urged on by the tales of richness and plenty in the Americas, Canada and Australia – and many died on the rotting coffin-ships that had no chance of surviving the wild Atlantic.

And the unlucky – or lucky, depending on the point of view – also embarked on a journey: the final one into Eternal Night. Those families blessed, or cursed, with a *banshee* grew accustomed to her bitter-sweet wailing, and the doors between this and the Otherworld remained open far longer than they should. The ghosts of the recently dead clung stubbornly to this world, and indeed, in some areas entire villages carried on a shadow-life in the twilight hours.

But wraiths of a different kind also walked the land as the suffering of a nation called forth the spirits of the past. Tall dragon-prowed, many-oared ships were sighted off the coasts; wild-haired warriors gave battle on lonely moors with misshapen beast-men; and tall, ethereally beautiful creatures walked the roads.

One other creature too went abroad, a creature from the Shadowland, a creature of the terrible times, the *Fear Ghorta*, the Man of Hunger.

*

Towards early afternoon the rain, which had been threatening all morning, finally fell, turning the already sodden fields into stinking pits. Eamonn stood there dumbly, watching the clay about his bare feet turn to almost liquid muck. Wearily he dragged his feet free of the mass and trudged on, his eyes glued to the ground, looking for anything – *anything* – edible. So far he had been lucky – very lucky; he had managed to find three fairly large potatoes, none of which showed any sign of blight. At the time he could scarcely believe his luck; the field had been scoured many times by others before him, but he guessed that the recent rains had brought them to the surface.

Twice that morning he had been forced to hide while packs of men and women roamed the fields, searching everyone's bag, and once he had struck out and knocked a younger and fitter looking man to the ground. The stranger had stopped him and demanded to know what he had found that morning and, without even stopping to think, Eamonn had hit him hard and with the last of his strength, leaving him retching on the cold ground, doubled up and clutching himself.

Eamonn looked up into the leaden sky, and allowed the cool water to run down his face, cooling his fever. He was twenty-two; he looked ten or more years older than that. Skeletal thin, the flesh tight to the bones on his face, giving it a skull-like appearance, and with only patches of hair clinging to his head, he looked like one of the walking dead. Only his eyes were bright and alive – and they burned with fever.

Then, having decided that the rain was down for the day and, keeping an eye out for the gangs of parasites, he set out for home.

There had been a partial failure of the potato crop – the

staple diet of the Irish peasantry in the nineteenth century – in the autumn of 1845. The result was that, in the following year, 1846, since much of the seed which should have been sown had been eaten through the hard winter, there was a smaller crop than usual, and much of what had been sown failed. All through that winter and on into '47, the famine was at its height, and what the hunger or cold didn't kill, the fever did.

Deirdre was waiting for him, huddled up against the wall hugging a tiny, almost rock-like crust of bread. The small one-roomed construction was cold, cold and damp Eamonn realised, as the stale earthen smell caught at his throat and lungs making him cough. Tiny flecks of blood spotted his hands.

Deirdre carefully handed over the bread, holding it like delicate glass, anxious not to let so much as a crumb drop. 'I got it today in the *toighthe-brochain*, the soup kitchen,' she whispered, her once musical voice now raw and hoarse. 'I saved it for you.'

Eamonn smiled his thanks and, soaking the bread in water, thoroughly chewed and swallowed the crust; it was like swallowing gravel. He opened his small bag. 'I was lucky today,' he said slowly, careful not to aggravate the coughing again. He pulled out some long grasses, nettles, a score of mushrooms and the three potatoes. 'We'll not go hungry tonight.'

'We must thank God for that then,' Deirdre muttered.

'What about the rent?' Eamonn asked. The rent was due, and although in some cases the landlords – usually absentee and living in either Dublin or Britain – had waived the rent, others were still demanding their due . . . and the rents were, more often than not, paid in kind: crops, potatoes, maize, turnips.

'I've heard nothing; but there was some talk in the

*toighthe* that they may be held over until next year.'

'That would be something,' Eamonn said quietly, 'but let's wait and see – we can only live each day as it comes.'

The night wore on and it began to rain again. The heavy drumming on the worn thatch above their heads kept them both awake, and they huddled together around the glowing embers of their tiny fire. Somewhere in the darkness of the room water was dripping, a dull monotonous sound that grated on the nerves and soon took on the likeness of a heartbeat.

They ate before dawn, using what little food they had sparingly, carefully hiding away one of the potatoes and a handful of mushrooms. They ate the potatoes raw, knowing it would give them a feeling of fullness, but their meagre rations did little for their hunger and only gave them cramps which left them both doubled up for almost an hour afterwards.

As the sky paled in the east Deirdre and Eamonn stood in the doorway of their pitiful dwelling and watched the sun come up over the tops of the trees. The sky flamed purple and grey and the colours gradually burned themselves into light, giving the day a delicate beauty.

They had been standing in the doorway for some time before they realised that there was someone watching them. Deirdre saw him first; she started and gripped Eamonn's arm, nodding to her right.

Eamonn eased his wife back into the room behind him and waited in the doorway until she brought him a long length of wood. He watched the figure carefully, squinting through the wisps of mist rising from the damp ground, trying to make out whether it was alone.

'What do you want?' he demanded eventually, when the figure made no move or sound. He winced as the shout tore his throat, and his voice sounded raw and harsh in his own ears.

The figure came forward. It was a man, although at first

sight that wasn't immediately obvious. He was almost naked and skeletal; his ribs were completely visible through the stretched skin, and his arms and legs were stick-like. The skin had fallen away from his face, leaving it skull-like, his eyes deep-sunken and shadowed, and his head was balanced on a thin scrawny neck. He took a step forward.

Eamonn brandished the stick. 'What do you want?' he repeated.

The creature's mouth worked silently, and then he croaked, 'Water.'

'Be off with you, we have none.' Clean water was as difficult to find as food.

'Water,' the stranger repeated.

'Eamonn,' whispered his wife, 'give him some.'

'We've barely enough for ourselves,' he hissed. 'And look at him,' he gestured with the stick, 'he's almost gone; giving it to him would be like throwing it away.'

'Give him some.'

Eamonn began to shake his head, and then he shrugged. He dropped the stick to his side and gestured to the stranger. 'All right then, but we don't have much mind ...' And then he smiled and sighed. 'But what we have I'm sure you're welcome to.'

The man came forward slowly, hesitantly, like a dog that has been beaten once too often and is wary of any offers of kindness. He smiled tentatively as he slipped past Eamonn into the room behind him, his eyes button-bright and shining in his corpse-like face.

Deirdre handed him a pitcher of water, instructing him to drink slowly, and then passed him the last potato. The stranger looked at it curiously, moving it round and round in his frail hands. He made two efforts to speak before any sound came out.

'You cannot spare this,' he whispered, his voice soft and gentle, like a lost child's.

'Eat it,' Deirdre commanded.

'But it is all you have.' The stranger's eyes began to burn brighter, feverishly darting around the room. 'You have nothing else; what will you eat ... and you don't even know me,' he said in a rush.

'We know that you are hungry,' Eamonn said quietly, 'and I doubt if one potato is going to make the difference between life and death for us.' He slipped his hand through his wife's and squeezed. 'Anyway, I don't expect we'll last through this winter.'

Deirdre said nothing, but squeezed Eamonn's hand and blinked back the sudden sting of tears.

The old man bit into the raw potato. The skin was hard and yellow, and the flesh bitter and foul, but he chewed his tiny mouthfuls thoroughly before audibly swallowing. 'You've lasted this long,' he said, 'surely you will last the rest of the winter?'

Eamonn smiled grimly. 'We have no food ...' he gestured at the empty pitcher, 'no water, no firewood, no turf, no crops. So even if we do live through this winter, we'll have no seeds to grow for next year, so we'll go hungry again and again the following year and again ...' Abruptly he stopped and began to cough, bright red blood spattering against the sleeve of his shirt. 'Like you,' he gasped, 'we are the walking dead.'

'Perhaps not.'

Eamonn looked up, and Deirdre gasped in surprise. The stranger's voice had changed, deepened, strengthened. And although the same half-naked skeletal figure was still standing before them, his posture had straightened and his expression had changed from totally abject to one of absolute confidence. He gestured with one long-fingered hand, and both Eamonn and Deirdre felt something ripple and flow through the room, immediately followed by a cold sharp gust of wind. The fire blazed in the hearth and when Eamonn turned around he found it was burning prime-cut turf, and he blinked against the pleasantly acrid odour of turf smoke which quickly filled the room.

'Who are you ... what are you?' Deirdre whispered, clinging to Eamonn.

The stranger smiled, his face no longer looking so skull-like now, but merely menacing and totally different. 'I am the *Fear Ghorta*, the Man of Hunger,' he said gently, his voice echoing and ringing inside their heads.

'What ... why are you here?' Eamonn asked, his voice a little above a whisper.

The *Fear Ghorta* shrugged, his bony shoulders moving visibly beneath the thin covering of skin. 'The time of famine is my time, for it is only then that I can walk in the world of men unnoticed.' He paused and continued in a different tone. 'I am of the Tuatha De Danann, and yet not of them. In their latter days, the People brought many creatures into existence, some pleasant and beautiful to look upon, but others ...' He shrugged again.

'We are the Guardians of this land,' he continued, 'and we are not without our powers. I have walked the length and breadth of Ireland these last two years, watching, waiting and occasionally interfering in the affairs of men. It is said that I bring famine, but that is not true; famine brings me, calling me forth from the ancient barrows of the Tuatha. My duties in these times are many, but my main task is justice. I have come across others like you: people willing to share their last crust with a total stranger, giving completely of their charity.

'But I have also come across others; people with plenty, hoarders, thieves and the like who will not even give the crumbs from their tables. And some are wealthy men, not needing the money or food, wanting nothing, but greed, greed rules aye, and will eventually destroy them.' The *Fear Ghorta* smiled again, showing his teeth, which were short and even except for the two incisors which were longer and pointed. 'And these I have been forced to deal with: a blight taking their crops of grain, a fire destroying their valuables or homes and, in one or two cases, leading them astray, making them cross a patch of "hungry grass". And you know, unless you eat immediately upon crossing the grass, you will remain forever hungry and could even die of hunger within that yellowed circle.'

The *Fear Ghorta* put the half-eaten potato on the table beside him and his long-fingered hand passed over it, and immediately it was whole again. 'No matter how often you cut this,' he said to Deirdre, 'keep a little back, and in a little while it will be whole again.' He pointed across at the empty pitcher. 'And that will never be empty.'

The *Fear Ghorta* turned quickly and slipped out into the morning, and was gone.


Deirdre and Eamonn survived the Great Famine. 1847 slipped into '48 and that moved inexorably towards '49 and '50. The young couple, by keeping a low profile, and using their magical gifts sparingly and carefully, rode out the worst of the hunger.

Eamonn stopped coughing blood, and when he eventually did get to plant seeds two years later they sprouted quickly and strongly, and he managed to reap two harvests.

They never saw the *Fear Ghorta* again, although they occasionally heard whispers of the skeletal stranger who roamed the countryside repaying kindness with kindness and pettiness in kind.

And in time the Man of Hunger returned to the barrows of the Tuatha De Danann and slept, and sleeps still ...

# Chapter Seven

# THE SEAL WOMAN

Declan Fitzpatrick climbed back up the rough beach, carefully picking his way through the stones, the sea-water on his bare feet already beginning to turn chill. The young man paused briefly on a smooth boulder before leaping across a deep pool onto the broad stretch of sand that ran up almost to the foot of the cliffs. He sat on the warm dry sand and dropped the heavy bag of cockles and crabs beside him and began to dry his feet with a scrap of cloth. He swore as he patted dry the rolled ends of his trousers – they would stiffen and stain. The sackcloth bag by his side suddenly twitched and a large crab scuttled out from it; it paused in the sunlight and then darted down to the beach, instinct directing it towards the water. Declan shouted and kicked some sand over the orange and bronze creature; it stopped and then darted away at a tangent. Declan scooped it up and, wary of the snapping pincers, carried it back to the bag. He knelt in the sand and shook the bag open before dropping the crab into it where it struck with a sharp click, which immediately excited another dozen or more snapping claws. The grey-eyed young man carefully appraised the day's catch – a couple of pence certainly, maybe even sixpence – before pulling the neck of the bag tight. He glanced up at the sun: it was nowhere near its zenith, and therefore still too early to head into town for the market.

Declan carried the bag to the nearest pool and slowly immersed it, and then he placed a heavy stone over the mouth of the sack to prevent it from opening. The salt water would keep his catch fresh until it was time to go. He then climbed up to his usual place: a small hollow in the cliffs, enclosed on three sides and open to the skies. Within, the ground dipped slightly and the sand was pure and clean, still warm from the early morning sun and sheltered from the tendrils of breeze that blew in off the broad expanse of Blacksod Bay. From where he lay he could just make out the seal caves that pitted the cliff-face across the bay, and he knew that behind him and to his right lay the small fishing village of Doogort at the foot of Slievemore. He made himself comfortable in the soft sand and, resting his head on his crossed arms, closed his eyes and slept.

The morning wore on and the sun turned the sea into a vast panorama of molten silver rolling against the warmer bronze of the beach. The wind dropped and the heat rose in shimmering waves from the sands, and one by one all the sounds of the seashore died: no gulls called or mewled from the cliffs, nothing crawled or scuttled clacking down the beach and even the barking of the seals was silent. Time stood still.

And then the smooth reflective water of the bay was disturbed by a series of ripples that moved steadily in towards the beach. Something small and sleek broke the surface for a moment, disappeared, and then almost immediately reappeared again. The water foamed and fell in molten droplets from the creature that rose up out from the water, a dozen more following in its wake. The thirteen creatures moved up towards the beach, the sun clothing them in silver and gold, and the heat haze distorting their shapes.

Declan knew it was late when he awoke. The sand beneath

his body was cold and hard and his little nook was in deep shadow. He lay still wondering how long he had slept – it must be sometime after noon by now – but perhaps if he hurried he might still make the market. He eased himself to his feet, feeling his stiffened muscles protest and his bones creak like an old man's. He rubbed the base of his neck and twisted his head to and fro; he could hear ringing in his ears … and then he realised that it wasn't in his ears!

Declan dropped to the sand again and pressed himself back against the cold wall; he could hear singing – or was it singing? It sounded like voices raised in conversation or laughter, but musical, so musical, and coming from the direction of the beach.

The young man lay flat on his stomach and edged his way towards the small cave mouth; this portion of the cliff was in shadow and he was reasonably certain that he could not be seen from below. He peered over the lip of stone and down onto the beach – and caught his breath in astonishment.

Twelve stately figures – men and women – moved slowly and fluidly around the central figure of a tall elderly man. The men were short and broad with dark glistening skin and short, tightly curled hair, while the women were taller and slimmer, their colouring lighter than that of the men and their hair longer and gleaming wetly in the sunlight. The old man standing in the centre of the slowly moving circle was almost as tall as the women, but his skin was cracked and seamed with a network of tiny wrinkles, and his short hair was silver-white.

Their mouths were moving and Declan strained to make out their words – and then he realised that the music he was hearing *was* their speech. It was low and gentle, almost like the sound of water over rounded pebbles, chattering, whispering, rich with the music of the sea.

He watched the circle break up into six couples, who continued to walk clockwise around the old man for a couple

141

of turns, and then each couple paused before him and bowed briefly before breaking out of the circle and disappearing in amongst the rocks.

Declan watched a couple lie down on the sand almost directly below him. Their movements were slow and stately, and they came free of their long cloaks with fluid ease. And then they began to make love in an unhurried, almost dance-like ritual.

The old man moved through the rocks and up the beach, his right hand moving in something akin to a blessing as he passed each couple and lifted up their shimmering cloaks. When he reached the last couple, just below Declan, the old man bent and murmured something to them; their laughter was light and studied, the sound like the foaming of the waves across weed. The grey-haired man walked past them and, almost at the mouth of the cave, stooped and arranged the bundle of cloaks on a broad flat stone; he then turned and retraced his steps down the beach.

A cloud slipped across the sun and shadow raced after him, leeching the colour from the sea, robbing the sand of its heat. Declan watched it coming and shivered with the chill, but he waited until the area directly below him was darkened by the swiftly moving cloud before making his move. His arm snaked out, groped amongst the rocks until it touched something cold and smooth, and then quickly withdrew it.

He sat back in the small cave and examined the cloth carefully. It was a large rectangle of brown-black, almost silk-like cloth with two tiny whalebone buttons at the throat. He ran his fingers through the short hair-like tendrils and felt its sensuous touch send ripples up along his arm. He held it up and what little light remained in the small cave ran like liquid along its surface and it was as smooth and supple as a length of rope.

It would fetch a pretty penny in Doogort.

He folded the cloak and slipped it inside the front of his shirt.


The stylised ritual lovemaking came to an end, and one by one the couples broke up and, first the men, and then the women, came and picked up their strange cloaks. They moved down the beach in a silent line and as they reached the water's edge they swung the cloaks up onto their shoulders and then threw themselves forward into the water. The mirror-bright waves foamed and splashed, hiding them completely and all that was visible was a triangular *V* cutting through the water towards the south.

But one remained; a dark-haired, dark-eyed young woman, clad in a long shift of almost translucent cloth. She stood silently over the spot where her cloak had lain, her eyes half-closed, her head tilted back and her broad nostrils dilated.

The young man shivered suddenly; there was something wild and elemental about her ... something terrifying. The woman's eyes snapped open, her head lowered and then she slowly turned towards the opening in the cliff. Her mouth moved and the strange liquid speech hung on the salt air between them. He didn't understand the words but the meaning was clear.

Declan stood, drawn out against his will. His hands trembled as they fumbled to pull out the gutting-knife from his belt.

The young woman smiled, exposing small pointed teeth and her dark eyes caught and mirrored the sunlight. Her arm came up, the green-tinged white cloth of her shift whispering as it slid along her bare skin, and she opened her hand. She spoke again, and this time the music seemed to blur and buzz within Declan's head, and he suddenly found he could understand what she was saying.

' ... *my cloak.*'

She took a step closer and Declan could smell her perfume; rich and sharp with the tang of the sea.

He took a step back and shook his head slowly. 'I . . . I have no cloak,' he mumbled through thickened lips.

'*Do not lie to me.*' The music which underlay her words was sharp and discordant.

'What ... who are you?' he asked slowly, suddenly barely able to formulate simple sentences. He shook his head, attempting to clear the muzziness which clouded his thoughts.

The music shrilled discordantly, and then lapsed back into words. '*Give me back my cloak foolish mortal.*'

Declan took another step backwards. His foot slipped on a smooth stone and his ankle struck against another. The sudden pain brought him back to his senses. His hand found his knife and he dragged it free and waved it in front of the woman's face.

She smiled. '*Your puny weapon does not frighten me. We have faced the spears and thunder-sticks of your people for generations; we have no fear left in us. All we feel for you is loathing.*'

'What are you?' Declan demanded. 'Where have you come from?'

'*I have come from a past age, a forgotten era.*' She blinked slowly and deliberately, and her eyes lost their metallic glint. She gestured back down the beach towards the waves. '*You saw?*' She nodded without waiting for an answer. '*You saw. Know then that we are the last of the Rón, the Seal Folk, banished to the waves when the last of the People of the Goddess fled the fields of man. I am Eán; give me back my cloak.*'

The young man slowly pulled the cloak out from beneath his shirt. The cloth, now shining rich and translucent in the warm sunlight, was warm and sensuous to his touch. He ran the back of his hand along it, and shivered involuntarily; it

144

was softer than the finest calfskin.

Eán's short, slightly webbed fingers reached for the cloak. Declan jerked it back out of her reach and menaced her with the knife.

'Why do you need it?' he asked, his voice surprisingly calm.

*'Once in every century we come forth from the seal caves to perform the Rite of Life, and consummate the sharing of life. Children born of the union will be like ourselves – creatures of both worlds, able to assume the form of man – but those conceived in the sea will be wholly of the sea. The cloak is our passport to this world of yours – without it, we would remain forever in the sea.'*

'It is very beautiful,' Declan said quietly.

*'It is.'* Once again Eán reached for the cloak.

Declan drew back and his eyes half closed calculatingly. 'There is supposed to be treasure in the sea,' he mused. 'Didn't some of the ships from the Spanish Fleet that sailed against Elizabeth sink in these waters? And were they not supposed to be carrying gold and precious stones? Well, young woman, if you want your cloak back you must be prepared to pay for it.'

*'It is beyond price,'* Eán said quietly.

'Nothing is beyond price,' Declan grinned. 'Bring me a gold bar or a handful of jewels and I will give you back your cloak.'

*'And if I do not?'*

Declan held up the cloak and almost gently brought the point of the knife against the material. He pressed and the cloth seemed to melt under the tip of the blade. 'Well then, I would be forced to cut your lovely cloak up into ribbons and sell them to the farmers and fishermen's wives.'

*'You are a cruel man, Declan Fitzpatrick,'* the young woman said quietly.

The young man started. 'How do you know my name?' he demanded.

145

'*You are known. You hunt the little creatures of the rocks and pools; you are known.*' She turned away. '*Come with me then if you desire your treasure.*' She walked down the beach, the slight offshore breeze moulding her flimsy gown to her slight figure. Declan, walking behind her, watched the muscles bunch and ripple beneath her tanned flesh and he felt his desire rising: he would have one other treasure he decided ...

Eán stopped almost at the water's edge. White froth foamed about her bare feet and across her slightly webbed toes. She turned to Declan and held out her hand. '*Give me the cloak now.*'

'What?' he demanded, 'and have you swim off and leave me standing here like an *amadan*. One of the first lessons we learned at our mother's knee was never to take our eyes off the leprechaun when you caught him; as soon as you looked away he would be gone.'

'*We are not the Earth Folk,*' Eán said stiffly. '*The Rón keep their word.*'

'There are very few who keep their word nowadays,' Declan said grimly. 'But before you go, at least give me a kiss to remember you by.'

Eán backed away, her eyes wide in fear or horror. '*I will be back,*' she insisted.

'Oh, I don't think so,' Declan said. 'As soon as I give you this cloak you'll be gone, and I'll never see you again. And since I won't be getting any treasure, you can at least leave me something ...' His large hands reached for her, but she pulled away and his fingers caught the flimsy material of her shift and it came away in his hands. He dropped the torn cloth and the cloak and lunged for her; she stumbled backwards and together they fell into the shallows. Eán gasped and the breath was forced from her body as Fitzpatrick forced himself on top of her. A wave washed in over them and the salt stung her eyes and bit at her throat. Fear and desperation lent her strength and she sank her

146

sharp teeth into his arm and pulled, drawing blood. He grunted in pain and struck out at her, but she twisted to one side and his blow only splashed the soft sand. Another wave washed in over them and Eán retched as she swallowed some of the salt water. In her present form she could drown.

The music was wild and disharmonious now, high, shrill and desperate. Declan was aware of it only as a mild discomfort at the base of his skull and along his teeth; he was far too intent upon satisfying his own lust.

And then the water boiled about them and Declan looked up into the face of a huge bull seal. It struck at him with large flippers, the blow rattling his teeth, almost cracking his jaw. Pain lanced through his leg as sharp teeth ripped through cloth and flesh. Another blow made his head ring and bloodied his nose, and then something struck him a massive blow across the chest sending him reeling backwards off the body of the Rón. He saw her scrambling up as he fumbled in the water for his knife ... and then a broad tail came up out of the water towards his head ...

It was almost sunset when he awoke, shivering and bloody. His face was puffed and both his nose and several of his teeth were broken. There was a sharp pain in his side whenever he breathed deeply, and there were two nasty open wounds on his thigh and shin.

Declan eased himself gently to his feet and stared across the darkening waters towards the seal caves dotted in the cliffs ... and counted himself lucky.

But in the end of course, the sea – or the Rón – claimed revenge. The following summer, during a particularly low tide, Declan Fitzpatrick wandered far out amongst the rocks in search of large crabs and other shellfish. And there he must have slipped on the weed-covered rocks, fallen and broken his ankle.

The tide washed his broken body ashore two days later.

# Chapter Eight

# THE CLURICAUN'S TALE

Will Slater stumbled over the cluricaun – literally! He was drunk again, and had somehow managed to wander off the road, but like most drunkards he had an innate sense of direction and he knew, somewhere deep within his pickled brain he knew, that if he kept his face to the sea breeze he would, sooner or later, arrive home.

It was a warm night, one of those September nights when the heat of the day clings to the ground, rendering sleep impossible and only dissipating close to dawn. Will had taken off his patched coat and carried it over his arm, the tails trailing in the dirt, the bottles in the deep pockets clinking pleasantly together.

He stopped in the middle of a field and pulled a squat, thin-necked bottle from his waistband, and attempted to guide it to his mouth. But he was swaying slowly from side to side and most of the whiskey snaked its way down his stubbled cheeks and onto his soiled shirt and waistcoat. The fat, middle-aged man gasped for breath as the alcohol burned his throat, staggered on – and fell. The bottle in his hand shattered and he cursed fluently in both Irish and English, but his fat had protected him from any real hurt and the only actual bruising had been to his pride. He sat up and dusted off his hands, and looked back over his shoulder to see what had thrown him ...

He was drunk. He knew he was drunk. He had set out that evening to get drunk; and he had succeeded gloriously. His calloused hands dug frantically in the pockets of his coat for another bottle, but his thick fingers only touched wet cloth and glass fragments. Almost absently he withdrew his fingers and licked the drops of alcohol from them. He blinked slowly and deliberately, closed his eyes, squeezed them tightly, and blinked again. And again.

His father had died from drink: he had seen purple and green snakes writhing up the walls and bloated spiders with human faces crawling across the bedspread before he had eventually passed on. But he had never seen one of the Little People, or more particularly a cluricaun. Will blinked again. But the cluricaun was still there; lying either drunk or asleep beneath a bush.

A cluricaun – sometime called a leprechaun. No bigger than his arm, dressed in a red waistcoat, green jacket, long green hose and wearing a pair of huge black brogues with enormous silver buckles. A black three-cornered hat covered the creature's face, slowly rising and falling with its breathing. A pair of tiny wrinkled hands were crossed over its breast, and a white corn-cob pipe had fallen from its fingers.

Will Slater's first thought was of gold. Cluricauns were reputed to have a secret store of gold, and all one had to do was capture and hold the creature and make it tell where the hoard was hidden.

He slowly heaved his great bulk off the ground and then crept towards the tiny creature. He was inclined to think that the mannikin was drunk; else why hadn't it woken up when he had fallen over it? He opened his coat, the odour of raw whiskey assailing his nostrils, and crept closer to the creature.

The cluricaun stirred.

Will threw himself forward and wrapped the sopping coat about the tiny man. He hit the ground hard and rolled over, holding the squirming bundle to his broad chest. He heard tiny cries of anger and rage which quickly became

149

slurred as the whiskey-soaked cloth enveloped the creature in an alcoholic haze. And by the time Will – now completely sober – reached his mean two-roomed cottage, the cluricaun was singing at the top of its surprisingly strong voice, and its ribald song even made *him* blush.

Sean Og awoke in darkness with the mother-and-father of all hangovers; he hadn't felt this bad since the last Shoemaker's Ball, and then of course someone else had been buying the drink, but last night now . . . He frowned, his face dissolving into a mass of wrinkles; last night? Well, but he'd be dammed if he could remember last night; if it had been a party it must have been a good one, for he couldn't remember a thing about it.

The cluricaun groaned aloud and sat up – and struck his throbbing skull against something hard and wooden. He groaned again, and tried blinking away the dancing coloured lights that swam before his eyes. He stretched out his foot, and the hard leather sole of his shoe struck wood, and when he reached out on either side his calloused fingers once again touched smooth wood.

He sat up again, more cautiously this time, until he felt the top of his balding head touch the top of the box – for that, he reasoned, was what he was in. He hammered on the walls, the sound booming inside the box, making his head ring. 'Oy, let me out,' he shouted, or rather, attempted to shout, but his throat felt as if it had been scrubbed down with soapstone, and it came out as little above a whisper. He tried again. 'Let me out.'

Will Slater awoke feeling sick, his head pounding in long slow waves. He had passed a restless night, dreams of wealth and riches drifting across his subconscious, bringing him awake every hour or so. He would be rich; he would have everything he had ever wanted, everything he had ever dreamed about ... and yet he still felt curiously dissatisfied.

He broke his fast hastily on milk and eggs, his red-rimmed eyes never leaving the small oaken chest into which he had thrown the cluricaun. He heard it awake and noisily explore its surroundings, and had listened to its tiny cries with a thin smile on his lips. He had ignored them.

It was almost midday when he returned to the cottage. Outside the sun was at its zenith and slowly peeling back the surface of the earth, exposing it like a gaping wound, and then bleaching it dry, discarding it and going onto another layer. Will stopped by the door, allowing his eyes to adjust to the dimness of the interior, feeling the sweat dry on his corpulent body. He waited, listening, and when he was sure that there was no sound from the box, crept across the hard earthen floor and knelt beside it. He was tempted to crack open the lid and peer within, but that he knew was what the cluricaun wanted. He rapped on the side of the box with his knuckles.

Sean Og came awake with a start, cracking his head once again against the lid of the box. He swore and rubbed the swelling atop the swelling on the crown of his head. 'Let me out,' he demanded.

'Never – at least, not until you give me your crock of gold,' the rasping voice amended.

'Never, at least, not until you let me out.' Sean Og smiled in the darkness. If the box were only opened for a second he would be gone, and then God help the Big Fellow who had captured him: he wouldn't have another day's peace for the rest of his life.

'Tell me where you keep your treasure,' the voice demanded.

'Let me out and I'll show you,' Sean Og wheedled.

'No!'

The cluricaun shrugged; that wasn't really playing the game. 'If you don't let me out now, I'll never speak to you again,' he said petulantly.

'Tell me where your treasure is and I'll let you out; otherwise you'll stay where you are!'

The cluricaun then made a suggestion as to where the Big Fellow could go look for his treasure and Slater, in turn, hammered on the box with all his might, making the creature's head ring.

And that was that.

Every morning thereafter Will would ask the cluricaun the whereabouts of his treasure, and every morning he would receive no reply. He knew the creature was alive; often he would hear the metallic tapping of a cobbler's hammer – although what the creature was working on was beyond him. Once he awoke to find the cottage dark with a thick pall of malodorous smoke; he panicked and jumped from his bed, and was half way out the door before he realised that it was coming from the box: the cluricaun was smoking.

It was about three years later that Will found the small stack of driftwood down by the shore. It was bright yellow wood, and the sea and weather had worked it into a variety of unusual shapes. He had carefully polished it with an oily rag and then taken it into town where he sold it to a visitor for a few pence. That evening the cluricaun laughed in his deep base voice, and continued laughing far into the night.

Will lost weight, and the excess skin hung in flaps on his face and body, and what little hair he had had fell out, leaving his head totally bald and skull-like. His watery eyes retreated into shadows, and he took to talking to himself. He still drank, but now he wasn't so particular what he drank, and took to buying a couple of bottles of locally brewed poteen from the hill farmers. It was deceptively clear – almost like water – but it would take the varnish off a table or scour rust from a piece of metal.

And then one day his brother came to visit, having heard rumours of Will's increasing ill health and haggard appearance. They had argued – which was usual – and Tomas fled from the house without even waiting for a cup of tea. Half-way down the path he slipped and broke his leg in two places. The cluricaun was laughing when Will returned from the doctor's late that evening and was still laughing when the sun rose in the morning.

As the years passed Will grew increasingly eccentric. He would often spend hours wandering the hills and marshes talking aloud, planning how he would spend his fortune. The townspeople took to avoiding him, for he had a violent temper, which was apt to flare up if he thought someone was even looking curiously at him. But when he was in his cups he would often talk of his treasure, his secret hoard, and although most people just laughed at the idea, there were a few who took the trouble to wander out to his cottage to investigate. And then the stories that Will Slater's cottage was haunted began to circulate. Voices were heard in the cottage, and sometimes a short ringing sound accompanied a bass singing, and occasionally puffs of curling black smoke would drift across the empty room.

And the townspeople shook their heads and some prayed for the lonely drunkard who had obviously been driven out of his wits by the spirit that was haunting him.

In the twelve years that Will Slater kept the cluricaun prisoner – after that first brief conversation – the only sound it made (except for the hammering, of course) was to laugh three times.


It was winter; one of the hardest winters Ireland had experienced in a long time. What crops remained in the fields were destroyed and the rivers and streams froze into solid blocks of ice. Food and fuel quickly ran short, and there were whispers of famine abroad ...

Will quickly used up what little fuel he had about the house and, with no drink left, he was forced to make the long journey into town. He was also forced to use a little of his savings. Some years previously, when he had realised in one of his sober moments that his drinking was becoming serious, he had buried some money in a small cask at the bottom of the field that abutted onto his cottage, and at the same time had made the resolve never to touch it except in the direst emergency. He had often been tempted, but somehow had always managed to resist that temptation – until now. Digging up the cask was back-breaking work, for the ground was like iron and the wood and metal of the spade and pick were so cold that they burned his hands. It took him nearly two hours to dig down the three feet to the money. There was nearly twelve pounds in the little cask – a sizeable amount for the time – but he only removed three and reburied the rest.

When he returned from town with his fuel, food and drink, the cluricaun was laughing again.

Slater was three-parts drunk and, tossing the wood and turf to one side, putting the bottles and parcel of food on the table, he crossed to the box and wrenched open the lid. His calloused hands closed on the surprised mannikin, threatening to snap him in half, and brought him back out into the cold light of day.

The cluricaun looked much as he had done almost twelve years ago when Will Slater had first stumbled over him. Perhaps his clothes looked slightly shabbier, and his hair and beard were somewhat longer, but his shoes still sparkled as if they had been made that morning – and perhaps they had, for the cobbler had little else to do.

Will held the struggling creature up before his face. 'In twelve years you've done nothing but laugh twice – and for no apparent reason – and I demand to know why you're laughing now!'

Sean Og smiled innocently and stuck his pipe in his mouth. Will grabbed the pipe and ground it into splinters in his hand. 'Tell me!' he roared, 'or by Christ I'll do the same to you.'

The cluricaun looked at the Big Fellow before him and sighed resignedly. 'Well,' he began conversationally, 'do you remember the first time I found something to laugh about?'

Will frowned and slowly shook his head; it had been so many years ago now.

'Ach, you remember,' the cluricaun said, 'it was that time you found that unusual yellow wood down on the beach ...'

He nodded, suddenly remembering.

'Well, that was part of the wreckage of a ship that went down off this coast a little over three hundred years ago. You probably don't remember, but there was a storm the night before: it carried the wreckage to the surface ...'

'I don't see ...' Will said doubtfully.

'One of the pieces you sold for a pittance was hollow,' the cluricaun paused and added in a slightly malicious voice, 'and it was filled with gold coins.'

Will felt his heart miss a beat and the blood rush to his face.

'The second time I laughed ... do you remember that?' Sean Og asked.

'When my brother fell,' Will muttered.

'Aye, when your brother fell and broke his leg. Now, if you and he hadn't fought, and he had stayed just a little while longer, he would never have fallen.' The cluricaun cocked an eyebrow at the Big Fellow. 'It's funny, don't you think?' He shrugged at Will's expression. 'Well, perhaps not then.'

'And now,' Slater said through gritted teeth, 'why were you laughing just now?' He was in a towering rage, the cords standing out in his neck and the veins in his temples throbbing furiously.

'You dug up some money this morning,' the cluricaun said. 'But you left quite a bit behind – and while you were in town a knacker wandering by, wondered why someone had gone to all the trouble of digging a hole in this weather and then filling it in, and so he investigated. Well, you can imagine his surprise in finding quite a little hoard ...' The cluricaun began to laugh again ... 'It's funny, it really is ...'

Slater screamed aloud, a red haze falling down over his vision. He flung the cluricaun to one side and raced from the cottage, down into the field. Half-way across the icy field he could see the disturbed earth, the black hole in the whitened earth. He was screaming aloud, although he didn't realise it; his heart was pounding furiously, and his head was threatening to burst with its throbbing. He stood over the hole and his clenched fists pounded against his sides again and again ...

Something flickered at the corner of his eye. He looked up to see the cluricaun casually walking past him, his three-cornered hat at a jaunty angle, a new pipe in his mouth. He paused and winked slyly at the Big Fellow. Slater felt the anger boil up and overflow within him; he threw himself forward after the creature, but his foot slipped on the ice-slick grass and he fell. He scrabbled to his feet, slipped and fell again ... His red tinged sight was now turning black at the edges. He slipped again and felt the pain ...


There is a local legend which relates how, on a winter's night, in the local churchyard, a cluricaun will come and sit on one of the headstones, and hammer incessantly on an already perfect shoe. But then, Will Slater was a 'character' in life, and it's not unusual to find that he still has something of the same reputation even after his death – which in itself is noteworthy. It seems he went wandering out into the fields without a coat on a bitterly cold day. He then fell into a hole and, although there is evidence to suggest that he attempted to rise to his feet, it seems he never succeeded. The cause of death was put down as exposure, but the

156

doctor's own report hints at something more, for in it he states that there was a look of absolute ferocity frozen onto Will Slater's face ... and what about the tiny footprints found in the snow beside him?

# Chapter Nine

## POTEEN

'Christ!' John Joe spat the clear liquid onto the ground. 'Tastes like piss.'

'Let me,' his brother, Paddy Joe said, leaning in over the rusted barrel and dipping a battered tin can into the bubbling mixture. He carefully brushed off the evil-looking froth and breathed in the vapour: his eyes immediately watered and his nose began to run. He sipped cautiously, and then copied his brother and spat the liquid onto the ground. 'By God, but that's a powerful batch you've brewed up for us now.'

John Joe nodded glumly. 'Aye, but we'll never sell it.' He ran his short stubby fingers through his greying hair. 'No one will drink the stuff.'

His younger brother chewed thoughtfully on a ragged thumb nail. 'Is there nothing you can do to it,' he asked eventually, 'add more sugar or something?'

'I suppose we can try.'

'Or ... maybe we could water it down,' his brother added diffidently.

John Joe glared at him; no one was adding water to his poteen!

The brothers were in the process of adding more sugar to the bubbling poteen when they heard the short shrill whistle from the field below the cottage: excise men coming!

They had about five minutes. The bags, bottles and cans

158

were tucked away into their respective hiding places, and by the time their youngest brother ran up, red-faced and out of breath, only the large bubbling vat remained. 'They're on their way up,' Micky Joe panted. 'Two of them; a couple more in the village. What'll we do?'

John Joe swore. They had a couple of gallons of almost drinkable poteen ready, and now to lose it all to a couple of nosy excise men ...

'We can't dump it,' Paddy Joe said suddenly. 'Micky, you hook up the tube and we'll drain it off ...'

'But there's no time,' Micky Joe said frantically, 'they're too close.'

'Then there's only one thing for it,' John Joe snapped and, putting his shoulder to the large drum, tipped it over. The clear liquid disappeared into the already damp ground and the bitter-sweet odour was blown away on the breeze. Micky Joe scuffed his foot on the sodden ground, rubbing away the ugly scum that had been bubbling on the top of the liquor.

And when the two excise men arrived five minutes later they found the three brothers industriously attending to the worn thatch on the cottage.

'Well, well, what do we have here,' John Miller said loudly to his companion. 'If it isn't John, Paddy and Micky Joe – and all working too ... probably for the first time in their lives I shouldn't wonder,' he added with a grin.

'A good day to you, sir,' John Joe said, climbing down off the roof. 'What can we do for you today, eh?' He looked at each man in turn. 'Could we offer you a little something, perhaps?' And then he added with a sly grin, 'There's tea freshly made, and there's some ice cold milk.'

John Miller turned to his companion, an older man with florid cheeks and a thick beard, smoking a pipe. 'As you can see, the MacCarthys are a hospitable lot.' He turned back to John Joe. 'But are you sure now you wouldn't have anything stronger about the house, eh?' He sniffed the air. 'Is that sugar I smell?' he asked innocently.

159

'That's God's own breeze,' Paddy Joe said quickly, 'blessed with the smell of turf and heather.'

'It smells like sugar to me,' the older man said quietly.

'The air always smells sweet up here,' John Joe said.

'This is Mr Ferguson, my superior,' Miller said to the three brothers. 'He is on a tour of inspection of this region. Can we go in?' he asked and, without waiting for an answer, entered the small evil-smelling cottage. John Joe hurried in after them, while the two younger brothers remained outside, frantically checking for anything that might give them away and implicate them in poteen making. But the only evidence that they could see was the soaking ground that squelched with every step and oozed clear 'water'.

Miller and Ferguson reappeared some moments later; Ferguson holding a large handkerchief to his face and even Miller, who should have been used to it, was looking slightly green. Behind them John Joe winked at his two brothers. 'Will that be all gentlemen,' he asked, smiling at their discomfort.

Ferguson nodded dumbly and concentrated on lighting up his pipe, attempting to dispel the foul odour that still clung to him with the fragrant tobacco.

'Have you been keeping animals in there?' Miller demanded.

'Aw sure, we're only poor country folk, we don't have room for cow barns and the like,' John Joe said slowly. Behind the two men, Paddy Joe began to choke with laughter, and his older brother glared at him. The cottage John Joe had shown the two excise men was now only used for keeping sheep in winter!

'It reeks,' Ferguson rumbled, puffing on his pipe, the glow from the bowl lighting up the waxed tips of his moustache. He struck another long match and pulled strongly on the flame.

'Aye, well ...' Miller said thoughtfully, 'I know you've been up to something, and I'll be back,' he warned.

'Oh, we'll look forward to that,' Paddy Joe promised.

'A good day to you then,' Miller snapped and turned away.

Ferguson allowed his gaze to drift over the three brothers in what he thought was a stern and warning manner, but which only succeeded in making him look like a short-sighted goat. 'Good day, then,' he rumbled and, turning away, tossed the match on the damp ground ...

Eight miles away in Aughacasala the townspeople heard what sounded like the distant rumble of thunder, but thought nothing of it; there was a storm due anyway.

# Chapter Ten

# THE CATSPELL

'You know he'll never marry you,' Grannia said to Sinead as
they crossed the field towards the house. The dark-haired,
dark-eyed young woman smiled secretly and whispered,
almost to herself. 'Oh, we'll see about that.'

'But he does not love you,' Grannia protested.

Sinead glanced across at her companion. 'But I love him,'
she stated flatly.

The older girl shook her head in exasperation, the fading
sun catching highlights in her reddish-bronze hair,
burnishing it to gold. 'He'll ruin you – take my word for it.
He'll end up marrying one of those fancy women in Dublin
or London; you're just a bit of a diversion for him on his
holidays.'

Sinead gazed dreamily up at the orange and black-tipped
clouds riding in from the west. 'Oh, but he's handsome and
kind ... and wealthy,' she added.

Grannia laughed. 'And why shouldn't he be; his father
owns most of the land hereabouts.'

'He'd make a fine catch.'

'But you won't catch him,' the older girl said finally.

Sinead's dark eyes snapped open, and Grannia felt a chill
wash over her, for they were flat and cold and merciless. 'He
will marry me,' she persisted, her voice low and hoarse, 'and
you can help me.'

'Me?' Grannia whispered.

'You can meet me tonight outside Leary's Pub, an hour or
so after closing time.'

162

'I can't; I won't be able to sneak out,' Grannia protested weakly.

'Of course you will,' her friend insisted, 'you've done it before – and you'll do it for me, won't you?'

'What are you going to do?'

'Oh, you'll have to wait and see. But come along tonight – and you'll dance at my wedding, I promise you.'


Giles Blackburn vaulted the low stone wall and strode across the hard, dry ground towards the cottage, whistling tunelessly between his slightly prominent teeth. He wasn't half-way across the yard when the cottage door opened suddenly and Sinead darted out, raced towards him and threw herself into his arms.

Giles staggered back and attempted to disengage the young woman. 'Steady ... steady on now,' he said pleasantly. He moved resolutely towards the open door, only too conscious that anyone could come along the road at any moment and, whatever his own reputation, he would do nothing that could anger his father – and threaten his allowance.

Once amidst the darkness of the tiny cottage however he kicked the door shut with his heel and, wrinkling his nose against the sharp, acrid turf smoke that permeated the entire room and clung to everything, he kissed Sinead deeply. His soft hands moved slowly up and down the young woman's back, feeling the smooth ripple of muscles beneath her thin cotton blouse. He held her close to his chest and he could feel the pounding of her heart against his ribs ...

With a gasp Sinead pulled away. In the semi-darkness he could see that her face was flushed and that she was breathing deeply. 'Why, I'm quite out of breath,' she panted, both hands going to her cheeks, feeling their heat.

'So am I,' Giles said, staring intently at her. 'You do that to me.'

She smiled, and for an instant Giles loathed himself for what he was doing. The girl was beautiful, very beautiful: a small, heart-shaped face surrounded by a mane of thick black hair, which matched the colour of her large, wide eyes. Her lips were full and red and her cheeks were glowing with health – and not the artificial colouring that city women were forced in many cases to use. She would make some farmer a fine wife ... and in a few years she would be old and fat, aged beyond her time with the bearing of too many children ...

The young man smiled sardonically; that was, of course, if she could find herself a husband once it became known that she had been friendly with the landlord's son.

'What are you smiling at?' Sinead asked quietly.

'At you.'

'At me? Why?'

'Oh, because I love you,' he said softly.

She stepped closer to him, and he could smell the corn sweetness of her hair and the freshness of her recently washed skin. 'Do you Giles, do you really?'

'You know I do.' He reached out and his fingertips touched her shoulder and began a slow descent onto the curve of her breast.

'And will you marry me, Giles?' she asked, a note of pleading in her voice.

His hand stopped. 'I've said that I will,' he said carefully, not liking the way the conversation was turning.

'When?' she demanded, a hard note coming into her voice. They had had this conversation before, and the answers were always the same.

'When we're ready,' he said cautiously. His hand moved fractionally lower.

Sinead pulled away. 'You've told me that before,' she accused. '"When we're ready ... when we're ready."' She swung around and faced him. 'Will we ever be ready?' she demanded.

Giles stepped back at the fierce light in her eyes. He forced a smile. 'Of course we will; time ... all we need is time.'

Sinead smiled bitterly. 'All you want is this!' Her hands rose and touched her small breasts through the cloth of her blouse. 'And what happens then? You'll no longer need me, nor want me. If you ruin me my father will throw me out, and I'll end up selling myself in the pubs or on the streets for the price of a meal – is that what you want?' she suddenly screamed.

The young man took her into his arms, and pressed her face to his chest, more to stifle her shouts than anything else. He stroked her long hair, murmuring softly as if to a child, and wondering frantically if anyone had heard her.

'Hush now, hush; I've said I'll marry you – and I will, in a while, in a month perhaps. I can't just now; I've got to work my way around my father, convince him that we really love one another. Look,' he said desperately, 'I'll take you up to Dublin in the next few days, and we'll pick out a fine dress and some shoes ... How does that sound?'

Sinead nodded dumbly. She slowly pushed away from him and wiped her eyes with the back of her hand. 'That sounds nice ... very nice,' she said quietly. He reached out for her but she pushed his hand away. 'No! I'm ... I'm not feeling well ...' And then she smiled through her tears. 'You can go now, but come to me tomorrow night. My father's going to town in the morning – and he usually stops in for a few drinks with his cronies; he won't be home till late. It'll be just you and me.' She smiled again and ran her fingernails down his stubbled cheek. 'Until tomorrow night then ...' And then she turned away and disappeared into the other room.

Giles waited a few moments to see if she would reappear, but then turned away and wrenched open the cottage door. He paused blinking on the threshold for a moment and then pulled the door closed behind him.

The young man strode jauntily down the dirt road towards the town. He would never understand women – and especially Irish women. One moment she was going on about her ruined reputation and the next she was telling him that her father would be away which would give them time together; he shook his head in wonderment.

He glanced back at the cottage. There was a small figure standing in the doorway and a white arm rose and waved him goodbye. He waved back and blew a kiss, smiling broadly in anticipation of the following night.

But if he had been able to see Sinead's expression, or the cold look in her dark eyes, then perhaps he might not have gone on his way so merrily.


Sinead touched Grannia on the shoulder and pointed. The red-haired woman started, and then squinted into the darkness in the direction of her friend's pointing finger. The moon slipped free of its covering cloud and illuminated the long row of mean cottages and tiny shops in silver and shadow. In the sharp light the young woman could see the low sleek shape of a cat slinking through the laneway opposite. There was a rustle of cloth by her side and then Sinead darted across the street towards the darkened lane. Grannia hesitated for a moment, and then gathered up her skirts and followed.

She found Sinead on her knees in the mouth of the alley, whispering sibilantly, an evil-smelling fish-head in her hand. For a moment nothing happened, and then the shadows moved and the cat came forward slowly, its back arched, treading carefully on its claws, the fur on its neck and spine rigid. It stopped before Sinead and spat, before darting forward to snap at the fish-head. Her hand closed about the creature's neck, catching the mangy fur and twisting it, pulling it up off the ground. The cat screamed and spat, its claws catching and raking her hand. Grannia fumbled with the rough sack Sinead had given her earlier, and held it open while her friend dropped the struggling creature within. Sinead then snatched the sack and, holding the mouth tightly in both hands, swung it hard against the wall of the alley. There was a sickening crunch and the sack went limp.

There was silence for a long time after that, and then Sinead turned back to Grannia, who was crouching back against the cold stone wall, her eyes wide with fear and her hands to her mouth. 'Go home now,' she said gently. 'It is done ...' The moon slipped free from the clouds and turned her eyes to flat silver discs. 'Forget what you have seen ...'

The red-haired woman nodded briefly, turned and slipped from the alley and down the moonlit street. She held her arms across her chest, holding herself, and she was shivering violently; for the killing of the cat had touched something deep within her, some primeval memory that whispered of magic!


'You're a fine cook, Sinead, I'll say that for you.' Giles leaned back on the hard wooden chair and loosened the buttons on his waistcoat. 'You'll make someone a grand wife ...' He coloured and stopped, realising what he was saying. But Sinead only smiled and turned away to the open fire.

'Would you like some more tea?' she asked quietly.

'Tea? Tea, yes, that would be nice.' The young man leaned forward and rested his elbows on the table as he watched her bend over the heavy black kettle, noting how her breasts strained against the thin cotton of her blouse and the glimpse of ankle beneath her heavy woollen skirt. He shook his head slowly and sat back, tilting the chair on its two rear legs, and stared up at the smoke and time-stained beams.

Sinead risked a glance over her shoulder, and then quickly pulled the small cloth bag from the niche beside the fire. Still rattling the kettle with one hand, she deftly pulled the drawstrings open with her teeth and poured the reddish-brown powder into the steaming water, which immediately took on a faint pinkish tinge. She poured the boiling water into the teapot and the coloration was lost as the tea darkened the water.

'I hope you like it strong,' she said, handing him a chipped china cup.

Giles nodded. 'The stronger the better,' he grinned, and then grimaced as the scalding tea burned his mouth – and the tea *was* strong with a brackish saline taste that was reminiscent of the sea.

Sinead moved slowly around the table and stood behind the seated man. She placed both hands on his shoulders and began to work her small hard fingers into the muscles. Giles tilted his head back and smiled up at her, feeling a sudden, almost overwhelming wave of desire rise up inside him. She leaned forward and kissed him, her lips briefly brushing his, sending shivers down along his spine. Sinead smiled and watched as his eyes began to glaze, and then she whispered a *word* into his open mouth ...

The young man convulsed, his muscles spasming and locking. The hair on his neck and the back on his hands rose stiffly, and the light of intelligence in his eyes died completely to be replaced by a blank glassy stare. Sinead smiled triumphantly down into his upturned face and waited until the last of the muscle tremors had ceased. She then bent forward and began to hiss insistently into his face. *'You love me ... you love me ... you love me ... you will marry me ... you will marry me ... you will marry me ...'*

'I love you,' Giles Blackburn repeated numbly, 'I will marry you.'

'I don't mind telling you that I think you're a charlatan, and that I'm wasting my time here,' Henry Blackburn snapped, his usually florid complexion now crimson and glowing.

'Then why are you here?' the old woman asked, smiling slightly at the other's discomfort in the tiny cottage.

'Because ... because ...'

'Because you're desperate,' the old woman said. She turned away from the large man and looked across at the woman sitting across from her on a low stool. 'Why have you brought Mister Blackburn here, Nora?'

The woman smiled shyly. 'Well, I'm the cook for the squire as you know, and he's in trouble, but being English he doesn't see it for what it is.'

The old woman slowly shook her head, her hard eyes darting from the large woman to the tweed-clad landlord. 'Start at the beginning, Nora,' she said gently, 'tell me what you mean.'

'You are Nano Hayes,' Blackburn interrupted, 'the local wise woman or witch or whatever you're called around here. My son – usually a sensible enough lad – has been acting very strangely recently, and has even gone so far as to propose marriage to one of my tenant's daughters ... a pleasant enough lass,' he added hastily.

'But not a suitable match for your son,' Nano Hayes finished.

'No,' the landlord said roughly, 'not a suitable match. I know something is wrong; Giles is a fine lad – high-spirited I know, but not foolish, and certainly not stupid enough to propose marriage to a country girl.'

'And especially not an Irish country girl,' the old woman added with a sly smile.

'That's not the point,' the Englishman said slowly. 'It's ... it's that he's not well ... he's not been acting himself recently.' He shook his head and spread his hands. 'I've tried everything, but the doctors say he's fit and well, and I know no one in the town is selling him drink.'

'You're not suggesting that because I have a certain reputation that I might have ... cast a spell on him?'

'What? Of course not!' Blackburn snapped, but the old

woman detected a note of doubt in his voice.

'And then again, he might just be in love with her,' she suggested quietly.

'What! Nonsense; he's already engaged to a very respectable young woman in London.'

Nano Hayes turned back to Nora. 'Why have you brought Mister Blackburn here; this doesn't seem like something for me.'

The fat cook wrung her hands and looked across at the old woman through eyes that were suddenly brimming with tears. In the dancing flames of the fire Nano Hayes looked thin and insubstantial, almost wraithlike. She had been old when Nora had been a girl – indeed, she had arranged Nora's match, and now she had three fine grown-up daughters, with two of them already married – and how old would the old woman be now? It was said that she had some of the *gentry*'s blood in her, and they were reputedly long-lived, but all she herself knew was that in her lifetime Nano Hayes had not aged one whit.

'You know Grannia?' she began quietly.

'Your youngest?'

'Aye, that's the one. Well she has been having terrible nightmares lately, and screaming about eyes and cats, bags and potions and weddings. I called in the priest, but he only blessed her and said it was tiredness and not getting the right food, and that there was nothing to be worrying about. And the doctor said the same.

'But a few nights ago I sat up all night with her. She was talking and crying in her sleep, and going on as if she were wide awake, and then I started to ask her a question or two – and, Mother of Divine God, but didn't she answer me!'

Nano Hayes nodded. 'That can happen,' she said quietly.

Nora leaned forward on the stool and her voice dropped to little more than a whisper. 'Nano, she spoke of her friend Sinead O'Dwyre catching a black cat and killing it by beating it to death ...' The woman's voice trailed off in horror.

The old woman sat back, her breath hissing through her yellowed and worn teeth. '*Aaah,* it becomes clear.'

'What becomes clear, what are you talking about?' The landlord pushed himself to his feet. 'Talking rubbish, absolute rubbish ...'

'Sit down!' Nano Hayes snapped, her voice cracking in the dim, shadowy room, and almost unconsciously Henry Blackburn subsided into his chair. The old woman turned her head and stared at him, her grey eyes large and glittering in the firelight. 'You are ignorant – and that excuses you somewhat, but do not let your ignorance blind you to the facts. However, persist in your stupid attitude and you will surely lose your son.' The old woman leaned forward and tapped him on the knee. 'You are lucky that Nora here is wise in the ways of the country; there are not many alive now that would recognise the catspell.'

'The catspell?' Blackburn said quietly.

Nano Hayes sat back in her chair and the shadows raced in and enfolded her, until only the pale oval of her face and her bird-bright eyes were visible. 'The catspell is one of the most ancient love charms known to man,' she said quietly.

'But ... but a cat!' Blackburn protested.

The old woman smiled briefly. 'Since the earliest times cats have always been associated with mystery and magic, and the ancients even had a cat-headed goddess. It is said that cats are not truly of this world; that is one of the reasons witches used them as familiars – the spirits from the Otherworld easily inhabited the body of the feline rather than something wholly from this world.

'It is possible to kill and cure with the body of a cat,' the old woman continued, 'and cats can bring both sickness and death and, under the proper conditions, carry it away with them. And if a woman wishes to bind a man to her,' she said, her voice barely above a whisper, 'then she will find a cat, a black cat, and slay it with violence but without touching it and in the name of the Evil One. The very life essence of the

171

creature is then dedicated to *him*, and in return the body and organs may be used in *his* name to work *his* will. The cat's liver or brain is then cut out and dried, and ground into a powder in the light of a full moon. Added to food or drink the powder renders the man open to suggestion, and then the woman works her will upon the man, holding and binding his soul and senses to hers.'

'Superstitious nonsense!' the landlord snapped, but there was a note of doubt in his voice and his eyes looked troubled.

The wise woman smiled. 'And yet you tell me that your son has been acting strangely recently, has professed undying love for this girl and, I shouldn't wonder, even threatened to take his own life if he is not allowed to wed her?'

The landlord nodded.

'And yet you claim he is a sensible lad!'

Henry Blackburn stared into the glowing coals for a long time before turning back to the old woman. 'Tell me what I must do,' he said quietly.

Giles Blackburn leaned back against the cold, damp wall sipping the scalding hot tea, watching Sinead dress. She smiled across the bed at him and then provocatively turned her back as she buttoned up her cotton blouse. She walked slowly around the rumpled bed and brushed past him, out into the cottage's only other room. Giles followed her, placed the chipped cup on the table and, wrapping his arms around her waist, laid his head on her shoulder. 'I love you,' he whispered, his breath warm and moist against her ear. She giggled and struggled around to face him, staring deep into his eyes, watching the light beginning to fade as the potion began to take effect again, dulling his senses, inflaming his lust. 'Marry me!' he breathed heavily.

'Yesss,' she hissed and pulled his face down on a level with hers.

The door of the cottage suddenly slammed inwards, crashing off the wall and coming loose from one of its hinges. The room filled with men, some of whom Sinead vaguely recognised. One grabbed her arm, dragged her away from Giles and sent her spinning against the wall, where she slumped down, dazed. Giles went for the knife in his back pocket, and then a short stick rapped him across the elbow, numbing his arm; another blow caught him in the pit of his stomach, doubling him up; and then another blow across the back of the head sent him crashing to the floor.

Henry Blackburn preceded Nano Hayes into the cottage. The landlord knelt by his unconscious son, and touched blunt fingers to the lump on the back of his head. He looked up at the man standing over his son. 'If you've harmed him ...' he warned.

'I've broken more heads than you've seen rents,' the man grinned, slapping the stick into the palm of his hand, 'and I know how hard to hit,' he added cheerfully. 'He'll wake up in an hour or so with a head the size of today and tomorrow.'

Blackburn looked up towards Nano Hayes. 'I can only hope you know what you're doing.'

The old woman came forward and looked down at the unconscious man. 'He'll be all right presently; lift him up now and take him back to his room. I'll follow along shortly.'

Four men came forward to lift the young man, when suddenly there was a scream from the other side of the room and Sinead threw herself forward, a heavy earthen pot in her left hand. She swung the pot at Nano Hayes, but she, with an agility surprising in such an old woman, stepped away from the blow, and one of the men struck the girl across the knuckles with his stick, and the pot flew from her hand and shattered against the wall. The girl then threw herself forward onto the man, but he casually backhanded her away from him, knocking her to the floor where she lay in a sobbing heap while the still unconscious Giles was carried out.

173

Back at the Manor Nano Hayes watched while Giles was undressed and laid on his bed. Under the watchful eye of both Henry Blackburn and his wife, she pressed a cold compress to the lump on the back of his head and then, opening her small bag, she removed a tiny glass bottle from a thick wad of wool. Henry Blackburn took a step forward and reached for the bottle, but Nano Hayes held it away from him.

'What is it?' he demanded.

'A ... cure,' the old woman said carefully. She held up the bottle and the liquid within sparkled emerald green in the late afternoon sunlight.

'Is it the antidote?'

Nano Hayes shook her head. 'There is no antidote to what he has been poisoned with. The drug he was given only dulled his mind, leaving it open to suggestion ... and there is nothing we can do to counteract that – except wait: time will heal him. This,' she held up the bottle, 'will only help him sleep and rest easy tonight and for the next few nights, until the actual potion has passed through his system. Like all drugs it must be renewed regularly, and from what you tell me Giles has been under its influence for some weeks now – he should be strongly addicted to it. He will need something to help him combat its effects.'

'But I thought you said that hitting him with the hazel sticks would help drive out the ... the ... the ...'

'Hitting him with the hazel sticks only nullified the spell briefly,' Nano Hayes explained, carefully measuring some of the green liquid into a half glass of water. 'As well as the potion, Sinead used an ancient spell to bind him to her. I used an equally ancient spell to counteract that part of it: the two opposites cancelling out each other.'

'What must we do now to keep Giles from that dreadful woman?' Mrs Blackburn asked quietly.

'He must be kept here, he must not be allowed to leave the room, and he must only eat and drink food and liquid that has been prepared in this house. He must have no alcohol and no fruit that is not from your own orchards. You must ensure that nothing he eats has been tampered with.' She bent over the bed and, lifting Giles' head, tipped a little of the green-tinged water down his throat.

'Is there anything else we can do?' Henry Blackburn asked.

The old woman glanced across at the couple standing by the door. She nodded briefly. 'Aye, there is one other thing you might do,' she said quietly. 'Pray.'

The first night Giles Blackburn ranted and raved, calling out Sinead's name over and over again, begging her to marry him. But he had been securely tied to the bed, and two of the landlord's men stood watching through the night. Nano Hayes came the following morning to administer the emerald liquid to the young man, who had by then fallen into an exhausted sleep, and that night he rested a little easier, although he still cried out Sinead's name. The third morning Giles was awake when Nano Hayes arrived, and he refused to drink the green-tinged water. The old woman smiled gently and shook her head, and then suddenly cracked her calloused hand across his face. While he was still shocked and dazed she held his jaws in iron fingers and poured the liquid down his throat.

And so it went on for four more days, but with Giles Blackburn becoming more lucid and clear-eyed with each passing day, until on the morning of the seventh day he actually swallowed the emerald liquid without a struggle. As Nano Hayes turned to leave, he said suddenly, 'I've been a fool, haven't I?'

The old woman turned back and smiled gently. 'Aye, you have, but we all make fools of ourselves at some time or another, and yours was not particularly of your own making.'

'The girl witched me, didn't she?'

Nano Hayes nodded. 'You could call it that,' she agreed.

'What will happen to me ... to her?' he asked quietly, looking down at his trembling hands.

'Nothing will happen to you, I should imagine. I should think however, that you will be sent back home or perhaps to the continent to recuperate. And in future,' she added with a sly smile, 'choose city-bred girls for your sport – or at least those with no knowledge of the country lore.'

'And Sinead; what will happen to her?' Giles asked.

'Justice is a mystery,' Nano Hayes said enigmatically, nodded briefly and left the room.


In a small country town it is almost impossible to keep anything secret for long, and the story of Sinead's attempted bewitching of the landlord's son was soon common knowledge. The local people, brought up in a staunchly Catholic country and with a horror of witchcraft, shunned the young woman, and in desperation she fled the town. Rumour placed her in Cork, and later in Waterford, but she never returned to her native town.

And some years later a small article appeared in the Freeman's Journal which, had Giles Blackburn read it, might have stirred some twinges of memory:

*The city coroner today passed a verdict of accidental death on Miss Sinead O'Dwyre. Miss O'Dwyre, of an address in Rutland Street, died from blood poisoning when she was bitten in the neck by her pet cat.*


But had Nano Hayes seen the article she might not have been surprised.

## Chapter Eleven

## THE BLACK CLOUD

It was back.

Seamus O'Rourke blinked away the sudden tears that stung his eyes, laid down the heavy bow-saw, crossed himself and began to pray. And although he was a tall, robust man, he was trembling like a whipped pup.

It had started some three weeks earlier. He had been clearing away the little field of scrubby woodland that bordered his strip of land, when he felt the chill fingers begin to trace their way down his spine and nestle in the small of his back and at the base of his skull. He was country born and bred, well versed in the country lore, and he knew without doubt that what he had just felt was a faerie blast. He shivered, and not with the cold, and made a mental note to leave a little something out on the doorstep for the *gentry* that night.

And then he had glanced up.

From where he was standing he could see the small white-washed cottage across the fields, with the diminutive figure of his wife moving to and fro outside it. But it was not that which held his attention: for directly above the house floated a thick black cloud. Seamus blinked and rubbed his hard hands across his eyes, but the cloud remained. It circled slowly above the thatched roof of the cottage, rippling and flowing as if disturbed by a strong wind, gradually drifting lower.

He felt the numbness begin then; sensation disappeared from his feet and slowly crept upwards, painfully encasing his legs in icy blocks. His vision began to darken about the edges, and startling splashes of colour darted across his retina. He fell forward onto his face, his legs now nothing more than slabs of icy stone ... and then the cock crowed.

The raucous cry cut through the morning air like the sudden rasp of a saw through wood, shocking the birds in the trees into flight, their cries and calls splintering on the air. Seamus immediately felt the excruciating return of circulation and his sight began to clear. The cock crowed again, and it seemed as if the whirling black cloud shivered like a piece of hammer-struck metal. And then the cock crowed for the third time. The cloud began to fragment, its dark colour lightening to a pale – almost white – grey and disappearing on the slight breeze that blew in over the mountains from the sea. Once again the chill fingers touched the fallen man, but briefly, like a feather touch, and then they were gone.

Seamus lay on the ground, his legs jerking and trembling of their own accord, his face spasming as pain lanced through the taut muscles of his calves and thighs. As the pounding in his ears subsided, he gradually became aware once again of the sounds of the morning: the wind whispering through the trees, the bird calls and the sudden flutter of wings, the creaking of wood and the paper-dry whisper of leaves across the ground. He also heard an irregular splashing sound which he realised was blood dripping from a burning scrape across his face. The old man rolled over and onto his back and breathed in the fresh morning air tainted with the distant tang of salt and the more fragrant odour of freshly cut wood. And he relished all the sights and sounds of that early September morning, for he knew he had just been touched by death.

*

178

It had happened again, some three days later. Once again he had been touched by the chill wind and then the cloud had gathered above his cottage and leeched him of his strength, leaving him numb and shivering as darkness closed in on his sight. And once again the cock had crowed three times, banishing the cloud.

And it happened again three days after that ... and again ... and again ...

But each time the cock had crowed and the cloud had disappeared.

By now Seamus lived in terror of the cloud, and every third day he would refuse to go out, and he remained indoors, drinking heavily. He lost weight and his features became haggard, his eyes sunken and lost. He took to watching the cock intently, and soon even began talking to the bird. And every morning when it crowed he would start from his bed with a scream.

And then, for over a week, the cock didn't crow and the black cloud didn't appear over the cottage, and Seamus began to hope that it was over.

But now it was back.


Marie O'Rourke jumped with fright when the cock crowed. She glanced across at the shadow of the sun on the floor: it was close to noon, and that bird had already crowed several times that morning. And she was getting sick and tired of it crowing at all hours of the day. She held her pounding head in her hands and then shouted at the bird standing on the window-ledge. It fluttered its tiny wings and crowed again.


It was worse this time. Although the cock had crowed twice now, the numbness was still there, whereas before it would have been clearing. His vision though *was* clearing, and he could see the oval shape slowly drifting away from the house.

Marie squeezed her eyes shut and concentrated on breathing evenly. She couldn't take much more of this. First there was Shea coming home every second day now, cut and bruised, and now he had taken to sitting inside all day and drinking, and when she spoke to him he either ignored her, or snapped back.

And then there were the Headaches. The doctor in the nearby town had told her that they were caused by worrying about her husband ... that they were nothing to unduly concern herself about ... and how long had they been married now ... over ten years and still no signs of any little ones ... well that's probably it then, a man of Seamus' age gets to worrying about heirs ... it will soon pass and everything will be fine ...

But the headaches persisted, and the crowing of the cock made it seem as if her head were about to explode. And on the window-ledge the cock puffed itself up once again, making ready to crow ...

One more time, if the cock would crow just one more time, then the cloud would go and the numbness would leave him. Just one more time.

The long-bladed, wooden handled kitchen knife neatly severed the bird's head just as it opened its beak to crow again. The blade buried itself in the window frame, and Marie fell backwards as the fountaining blood splashed over her. The bird's wings fluttered and its nails tore into the woodwork before it tumbled over and fell into the room, where it was quickly surrounded by a thickening pool of blood.

The cold slammed into Seamus like a fist, driving the breath from his lungs. It hammered at the base of his skull and encased his spine in a leaden sheath. The cock, if the cock crowed ...

The cloud above the cottage solidified into a dark whirling oval, and then, as Seamus looked up, it began to fragment, like wind-blown smoke, but leaving wisps and tendrils still hovering over and about the cottage. Seamus blinked, blinked again as his vision darkened, and then he cried aloud, for the remaining pieces of the fast disappearing cloud were taking on a shape. He squeezed his eyes shut, but when he opened them again the images remained: images of his long dead parents and brothers.

'Dearest God ...' he breathed. The chill abated somewhat when he spoke the Name, and he staggered to his feet, and then, half walking, half crawling he staggered across the fields towards his cottage.

Inside he found his wife sitting on a straight-backed wooden chair, her head buried in her hands, her tears staining the wooden table. Seamus leaned against the door frame, watching the colours dance before his eyes in time to his pounding heartbeat. 'The cock ...' he gasped.

Marie gestured wanly towards the window.

Seamus fell across the room towards the window, clinging tightly onto the few pieces of furniture and the walls. He sank to his knees beside the headless cock, and then turned to stare up at his wife. 'Woman,' he whispered, 'you have killed me!'

It was some days before anyone from the nearby town

chanced to pass by the lonely cottage. As is usual with country folk they turned off the road and took the winding path that led up to the cottage, to pass a few words with Seamus and his wife.

They found Seamus O'Rourke lying dead beside a decapitated cock, and while there was plenty of blood, none of it seemed to be his. They also found Marie O'Rourke lying asleep in the bed in the next room. And when they woke her they found she was quite mad, and she talked incessantly of cocks crowing ... and a dark cloud ... and the cold ... the terrible cold.

And when the story went around the town, those wise in the country lore nodded their heads sagely, for hadn't they warned Seamus about clearing that patch of scrubland that touched on his fields, for wasn't it sacred to the *gentry*, and wasn't the Black Cloud of Torment one of *their* own special punishments?

# Chapter Twelve

# THE CARD PLAYER

The last of the late night revellers had gone and the fire burned down to smoking embers, but still the four men continued playing. Behind the wooden counter the barman dozed on a high chair, a half finished drink before him, an empty bottle by his feet. The pub was silent except for the occasional rattling snore from the barman and the greasy-slick pat of the cards as they fell onto the stained table. The four men hadn't spoken now for over an hour; the cards spoke for them, and tiny movements of their hands, or a nod conveyed whole sentences. There were a dozen empty glasses on the floor and half that number again on the table, some with drink still in them, but long since gone flat.

Three of the players were obviously brothers: dark-haired, dark-eyed, with the same bone structure to their faces. They were dressed in rough working clothes, patched and worn, and carried with them an odour of fresh clay and sweat. Their hands were calloused, the nails dirty and broken, but they handled the cards as if they were delicate crystal.

The fourth player was totally different. He was taller than the brothers and almost excessively thin. He was dressed in a shabby black suit with a soiled white shirt and stained tie. And yet his iron-grey hair was neatly combed and gleaming and his short square-cut beard was carefully trimmed. His hands were long and thin, the nails clean and rounded, and he handled the cards with practised ease.

The four men had been playing for nearly four hours now and what for Colm, Diarmuid and Padraig had started out as a bit of sport had by now turned deadly serious, and they were playing with an almost frightening intensity.

The three brothers had been playing quietly together at their usual table in the corner of the room, when the stranger had come over and asked if he might join them for a couple of hands. Glad of the company they had agreed, and drank his health in the beer he bought. The stranger had lost steadily at first, small amounts to each of the brothers, but enough to excite their interest in the game. And then he began to win; a hand here and then another, and then he would lose one, win one, and win again. And slowly, but surely, he was winning steadily.

The brothers lost back what they had won earlier from him, and then they began to lose their own money. Occasionally one or other of them would win a hand, but only to lose it again quickly.

And the stranger, unlike the brothers who would immediately pocket their winnings, left what he had won on the table: an enticement and lure.

The night wore slowly on into morning, and gradually the sky to the east began to lighten in anticipation of the dawn. And the brothers had little else to lose.

The stranger laid his cards face down on the table. His sharp eyes touched each of the brothers in turn, and then he smiled. 'Well?'

Reluctantly Colm fanned his cards and dropped them onto the table, followed by Diarmuid and Padraig. The stranger smiled again. 'My hand wins,' he said quietly.

'Again,' Padraig said ominously.

'Perhaps once too often,' Diarmuid added.

'You've just about cleaned us out,' Colm said quietly, 'we don't have much left to wager.'

The stranger smiled, the corners of his mouth twisting upwards, but his eyes remaining cold and hard. 'You have your lands, your house ... your souls. You have not lost everything.'

'If you think we're going to wager our land or house well ... you've got another think coming,' Colm said quickly.

The stranger touched the pile of money before him. 'How much would you make in a week,' he asked suddenly, 'three pence, sixpence, a shilling, two shillings? There is – *what* – five pounds here. Well, let's make it double or nothing.'

'But we cannot,' Colm said, 'we can't afford it.'

'How much would you say your land is worth?' the stranger persisted. 'Five pounds ... ten pounds; let's say ten pounds. I'll advance you ten pounds against the price of your land.'

'No!' Colm snapped.

'Yes,' Diarmuid and Padraig said quickly. Padraig turned to his older brother. 'What if we win?'

'What if we lose?'

And so they played another hand – and lost.

The old man smiled again. 'Let us now say that there is fifteen pounds on the table: five of mine, ten of yours. What else can we wager on?'

'We have nothing else,' Colm said forcefully. 'You have taken our land; what else does that leave us?'

'Why, your cottage of course. And how much is that worth?' He waved the question aside with his hand. 'Well, let's say ... fifteen pounds shall we?' His eyes were flat, blank and unblinking, like a reptile's. 'Shall we play?'

There was something manic about the game now. Each of the brothers felt that the initiative had been taken away from them, that they were little more than puppets being manipulated. To gamble everything: money, lands, cottage, and for such huge sums was absolute craziness, pure madness, folly ... and yet they continued playing.

The old man dealt the cards with practised ease, his fingers seeming barely to move, yet sending the paste boards skimming across the table to land, face down, before each brother. The atmosphere was electric as they slowly examined the cards – and the game continued.

They played – and won!

One moment they had nothing, and the next everything again: house, lands, money. It took a moment for the truth to sink in, but before they could react the stranger said calmly, 'Double or nothing?'

Something inside Colm screamed, *No ... No ...* but he found himself carefully shuffling the slick cards and slowly dealing them around the table. Double or nothing.

And so they played and they lost.

The old man smiled, and this time his whole face lit up. 'You can pay me what you owe me now,' he said quietly.

'We cannot,' Colm said numbly, 'we don't have that sort of money.'

'Oh dear ... But you do of course acknowledge your debt. But naturally this man is a witness to it all ... is that not so?' He swivelled around in the chair and looked across at the barman, who was wide awake and staring in amazement at the small group. He glared at the brothers.

'You're mad; what in God's Holy Name have you done? By Christ, you've sacrificed your house, your land ... and to what? A vagabond, a worthless tinker ...'

'Have a care my man,' the stranger said coldly, 'you may regret what you say. And bear in mind that you were a witness to what happened here tonight.'

'You *amadans*,' the barman suddenly shouted, 'he might as well own you now.'

The old man nodded seriously. 'I do own them.'

Colm began trembling violently, the gambling fever beginning to fade and realisation setting in. What about their mother ... where would she go, what would happen to her ... what would happen to them? It was the workhouse for paupers. He bent down to pick up his drink. The floor beneath the table was littered with bottles and glasses, clumps of earth and turf. He saw his brothers' bare feet, one twisted around the legs of the chair, the other firmly on the floor, and ... something else!

'*Jesus God!*' He erupted upwards, sending the table toppling over the stranger, and pushing his two brothers backwards at the same time. Glasses shattered and then a line of bottles behind the barman exploded one by one. The embers in the grate flared and the gas lamp blazed as an icy wind whipped through the empty pub. The lamp swung wildly on its chain before exploding into a ball of flame, but luckily most of the flames died on the damp earthen floor and the barman quickly beat out the others. The windows – with their thick bubbled glass – cracked and the door was ripped off its hinges and cannoned through the small room, crushing tables and chairs beneath its weight. And then the wind died as suddenly as it had begun.

There was silence in the pub for a long time after that, the only sound the steady dripping of alcohol from the shattered bottles. When the barman eventually did light a candle, he found the three brothers lying huddled beneath the overturned tables and chairs. The stranger was gone, but there was a stench of burned wood. On the underside of one table that lay directly across the door they found two cloven hoof-marks burned into the wood.

# Chapter Thirteen

## THE LAST OUTPOST

Between the shadowland of night and dawn the old magic still lingered, touching the mound with the ancient mystery that had once claimed the entire island. And in a way it was now an island, a relic from the distant past drifting serenely into the present and an uncertain future.

'What do you mean, they refuse to flatten it?' The American accent was raw and harsh on the chill morning air.

Michael Hughes smiled tightly, mastering his growing anger. 'The workmen have refused to level the fort – *that* mound.' He pointed across the hedgerows towards the low mound rising out from the morning mist which clung to the damp fields.

'Is this a goddam strike or what?' the small, dark American demanded angrily, colour beginning to seep into his cheeks.

'No, Mr Weiss,' Michael Hughes said evenly, no longer smiling now. 'It is not a strike. That hill is an ancient burial mound, a faerie fort, and for starters the workmen – Irish workmen remember – are extremely reluctant to bulldoze part of their national heritage ...'

'National heritage crap!' Weiss snapped.

'And secondly,' Hughes continued in the same even tone, 'it has a certain reputation. It is a faerie fort and they believe it would be unlucky – if not downright dangerous – to attempt to interfere with it.'

'What is it?' Weiss demanded. 'More money? Do they want more money? Give it to them! We're already four weeks behind schedule, and in five days' time there's a quarter million dollars worth of prefabricated buildings and equipment coming in here. I want an empty – *flat* – field to put it in. Is that understood Mr Hughes?'

'It's not the money,' Michael said quietly, 'they really believe that if they bulldoze the fort then something bad will happen.'

'If they don't bulldoze that ... that fort, then something bad will happen!'

Michael looked down at the angry strutting man, ridiculous in a three-piece suit with the trousers tucked into a pair of high green boots. 'And what do you mean by that?' he asked quietly, his breath pluming on the cold air.

Weiss looked up slowly. He smiled at the younger man, his lips drawing back from his too perfect teeth and his eyes remaining cold. When he spoke his Brooklyn accent was more pronounced. 'Then I think that my company which, I might add, has invested a lot of money in this project which would undoubtedly benefit this underdeveloped region, would be forced to reconsider its investment.' He finished slightly breathlessly and smiled triumphantly.

Michael Hughes shook his head and smiled. 'Mr Weiss,' he said slowly, and with something like pity in his voice, 'you have neither the power nor the authority to make such grand sweeping statements.' His voice changed slightly and took on a touch of humour. 'Whatever you may like to think yourself, you are little more than a sites manager.'

The American's face turned livid. He raised his hand and pointed his fingers at the younger man's face. 'You ...'

'Your company,' Michael continued, 'stands to make a sizeable profit from this site, and it will also benefit from the numerous concessions that the Irish Government offers companies like yours which decide to invest here.'

The American visibly mastered his anger. He stepped

closer to the Irishman, and Michael could smell the nauseous odour of stale beer on his breath. 'And all you have to do, boy, is to act as a go-between; I'll take no crap from you. Back in NY ...'

'But we are not in New York,' Michael said calmly, 'we are in Ireland, and we do things differently here.'

Weiss suddenly changed tactics. He had become conscious that many of the workmen had gathered around and were listening intently to the argument. 'Mr Hughes, I am making a formal request that you ask your men to bulldoze that hill,' he said icily.

'They have refused.'

'I will, of course, be forced to make a full report on this matter,' Weiss said stiffly. 'What reason shall I give for their refusal to work?'

'They have not refused to work; they have refused to flatten that mound ...'

'What reason, Mr Hughes,' Weiss persisted.

'Fear, Mr Weiss,' Michael said, turning away, 'fear.'


When the world was young and magic and mystery still abounded; when the lands themselves were not fully shaped; when the creatures of imagination walked the fields and monsters ruled the depths of the new oceans, then the gods walked this world and communed with the sons and daughters of man. And some came across the seas in their great glittering ships that were of metal and precious stones. These were the Tuatha De Danann, the People of the Goddess, and gods themselves in their own right, and their power and majesty held sway over the small emerald isle for generations.

The Tuatha defeated many enemies and scoured the land of evil, but in the end they fell to the slayer of all gods: time. And slowly the power of the Tuatha was eroded away. New gods rose and came to prominence on the island, and foremost amongst these was the One God, the Christ. The people gradually forgot the gods of their forebears and the People of the Goddess became as other lost gods: more than mortal, but less than divine.

And so they retreated to the Secret Places: the hidden valleys, the Lands Beneath the Waves, the Magical Isles and the Worlds Below. Their numbers dwindled, but they survived in myth and legend as the Shining Ones, the Sidhe, the *gentry*, and time and ignorance confused them with their servants, the Dark Folk, and they became collectively known as the Faerie Host.

But they lived on.

And some remained in the Worlds Below, which could only be entered through the Faerie Forts.


Michael held the telephone a few inches from his ear and allowed the irate voice to drone out into the empty room. When there was a pause he put the receiver back to his ear. 'All I know,' he said patiently, 'is that the workmen have refused to bulldoze the mound. It's an ancient artifact, a local attraction ... Yes sir, I know there's a lot of money at stake here...' He paused and listened again. 'Look,' he said finally, 'there is nothing I can do. I've spoken to the men and I've met with a point blank refusal ... They've refused offers of more money, and they laughed when I threatened to fire them. And at the moment,' he added, 'they are in touch with their local T.D. in an attempt to have this whole project stopped – or if not stopped then at least relocated, and yes, I do know how much that would cost.'

There was silence at the other end of the line and then it abruptly went dead. Michael slammed down the receiver. What a mess: it was blowing up out of all proportion.

He had known something was brewing for the past few days. The workmen – locals employed under the direct labour scheme – had been growing increasingly nervous as the fields on either side of the low mound had been cleared and levelled, and he had been asked on more than one occasion whether they were actually intending to flatten the mound. He had answered cautiously that it was in the plans, but the workmen had only smiled and said that they were sure that he was only joking, and sure why would he want them to do something like that ...?

But that morning, when he had instructed the foreman in the day's work schedule – which included the levelling of the fort – the men had refused to work.

The phone rang again, but it was probably Weiss, checking to see if he had received that call from Dublin. He let it ring.

Outside the sun had burned off most of the mist, leaving the ground fresh and sparkling as if it had been dusted with broken glass. Although the window had been painted shut a long time ago, he could still smell the morning freshness of the air. He could see the tops of the trees moving in the breeze blowing in from the west, and low clouds scudded across the clear sky. From where he stood he could see the top of the mound over the roofs of the cottages opposite the hotel and across the hedgerows. To the south of the mound the land looked curiously bare; no hedges bisected the fields, no trees clumped together in the corners of the same fields ... there was nothing. Nothing except the garish yellow of the diggers and the drabness of the trucks in the flattened fields.

What price progress, he asked himself.

It was some time after eleven, and the trucks and diggers should have been moving and the air above the fields filled with shouts, the roar of engines and a thick blanket of dust. But there was no movement, no sound, and the only dust in the air was that which had been raised by the wind.

Karl – Carl, since he had long since dropped his Polish

connections – Weiss walked slowly around the low mound, his green rubber boots squelching in the sodden ground. He had been around the mound twice now, and he still could see nothing special about it, but the locals believed it to be a faerie fort, a burial mound, a barrow and God knows what else ... and they refused to dig it up. His own parents had come from one of the most superstitious stock in Europe, and they had carried their superstitions with them into the New World, but at least time and exposure to the twentieth century had rounded off some of their peasant edges. These Irish ... Christ, but some of them were still living in the last century.

The city people were all right, they at least knew which side their bread was buttered. But these country people ... The small dark American smiled ruefully; the thing was he had dealt mainly with country people when he had been negotiating this deal, and by God, but they were sharp! It was a country of contrasts ... and complete unpredictability.

He scrambled up the low mound, bending almost double and using the long wet grass to help himself upwards. It was at times like this that he remembered that he was no longer a young man. He dug his heels in and paused, pulling out a white handkerchief and mopping his face, while he allowed his heart time to slow down somewhat; his doctor had warned him about overtaxing himself. His rubber boots slipped with a squeak on the wet grass. With a sigh he put away his handkerchief and heaved himself upwards, pulling on the tufts ... and then he swore as a thin line of fire ran across his palm. He pulled out his handkerchief again and wrapped it across the long grass cut: this was not going to be his day! But he persisted and climbed up to the crest of the mound and stood there for a while, staring out over the fields, flat and dark and ugly to the south, the raw earth showing through like an ugly festering wound, contrasting sharply with the lush greenness to the north and east, and with the splash of colour of the houses to the west. He breathed in the fresh, clear air – and coughed. He missed the city smog.

Unnoticed by him, the blood from his cut palm seeped through the cotton handkerchief and dripped onto the ground, soaking into the grass.


Michael Hughes paused by the hotel desk and handed in his key. Dave Conlon grinned sympathetically at Michael's expression. 'You've had a hard morning of it, I hear.'

'News travels fast,' Michael said quietly.

'Ah sure, I didn't need to be told; I knew the lads wouldn't touch the fort.'

'Well, I wish you'd told me,' Michael said ruefully.

Dave Conlon grinned. 'Sure I thought you knew.'

Michael shook his head. 'I thought the men were having a bit of sport at my expense; I didn't think they were serious when they said they wouldn't touch the fort.'

'But you should have known.'

'How could I ... born and bred in the city, remember?'

Dave shrugged. 'Aye, well I suppose you're not as well up in the country lore in the city.'

Michael leaned across the polished wooden counter. 'Tell me why they won't flatten the mound then?' he asked. 'What's the significance?'

The small balding man folded his newspaper and laid it to one side. He took off his glasses and polished them on a scrap of cloth. 'Well now, you see, that fort goes back a long way, it's one of the reasons this town is here; you see, the town – it was a village then – was built beside the fort, so that the villagers would always be under the protection of the faerie folk. Down through the years many stories have grown up around that fort. I don't know the half of them, but old Matt, who drinks in Nelligan's, the pub next door, would be able to tell you quite a few if you were interested. He's related to an old witch who used to live around here, a

Nano Hayes, and her name is always connected with the fort.

'It's said that the last of the faerie folk live beneath the mound, and once, in my grandfather's time I think, they even found the body of a young girl lying at the foot of it one bright November morning, just after Hallowe'en.* The story goes that she was taken by the Sidhe for spying on them.' He shrugged. 'It's just a story, but sometimes, when the moon is full, you can hear all the dogs in the town howling and baying out in the direction of the mound ...'

Michael caught the twinkle in the other's eye and laughed. 'Why you ... I may be from Dublin, but I am Irish, and I can smell a story like that a mile away.' He paused and added quietly. 'However, you might try it on our American friend.'

Conlon grinned. 'I already have. He wasn't too keen on it either. Ah, but he's a sour puss ...'

'Where is he now?' Michael asked, suddenly interested.

'Oh, he's out. He left here some fifteen minutes ago, cursing and swearing like a trooper.'

'Where did he go?'

'He headed off down the street. He's probably going to the workings; he had his boots on.'

'Thanks.' Michael ran from the small hotel and darted across the street, squinting against the hard morning sunlight that reflected back from the whitewashed cottages and colourfully painted shops. He cut down a side street between two thatched cottages and then across a second, smaller street and down a lane between the newer shop buildings and out into the fields. He swore as he sank up to his ankles in the soft mire, the liquid muck seeping in over the tops of his shoes and staining the ends of his trousers. He kept to the edge of the fields and skirted the worst of the desolation, remembering the fields – clean, fresh and green

* see 'Into the Shadowland' *Irish Folk and Fairy Tales vol. 1*

– as they had been barely three weeks previously. The new project had certainly brought prosperity to the small country town, but the price had been high.

He met Weiss close to the foot of the mound. The small American was red-faced and covered in a light sheen of sweat. Strands of hair, which were usually trained across his balding head, hung down by the side of his face, giving him a curiously decrepit appearance. His pin-striped three-piece suit was stained and rumpled and there were dark patches of thick mud on the knees. He was holding his left arm awkwardly and there was a blood-soaked handkerchief wrapped around his hand.

He walked right past Michael without saying a word, and then he stopped abruptly. Without turning around he snapped. 'You get that mound levelled Mr Hughes, or I'll bring in my own men and do the job myself.'

Michael stood in silence watching him make his way across the field. He didn't doubt that the American would carry out his threat and bring in outsiders. How would the townspeople react then, he wondered? He shivered, suddenly realising how cold it had become, and turned up the collar of his light jacket, tucked his hands into the pockets and followed the American back across the fields towards the town.


Time had passed the mound by. It had been old when the followers of the New God had come in their frail crafts to the island's shore, and later, when the yellow-haired and pale-eyed Northerners devastated much of the surrounding countryside, they had left the mound alone.

Armies had camped in the fields around the mound, time and custom changing their clothing and weaponry, although in many cases the cause remained the same, but curiously enough they never actually camped on the slopes of the fort, nor posted lookouts on its crest, although it commanded an excellent view of the surrounding fields. For although the De Danann were gone, their magic and mystery remained, and time had enhanced the legends.

A blast of cold air whipped in around him as Michael pushed open the door to the pub. He stepped inside quickly and brushed off the worst of the rain onto a large rush mat before shrugging off his coat. Although he had only run in from the hotel next door he was soaked through.

The change in the weather had come on quickly, with a cold front moving in from the north, bringing rain and sleet with it. A razor wind cut down through the town's broad main street and whistled through the alleyways, and the only creature moving outside was a bedraggled stray.

The pub was warm and close, a huge open fire burning at one end of the room; shaded, low-wattage bulbs giving everything a faintly dusky appearance. Heads turned in his direction, nodding briefly before turning back to their drink or conversation. Many were from the works, others were local farmers, shopkeepers or the townspeople. Conversation was low and muted with a sudden shout of laughter rising briefly before sinking back into the general murmur of the room. Michael made his way around the small circular tables to the crowded bar, nodding at people he knew. He ordered a pint, and leaned back against the polished wooden bar sipping the dark white-headed Guinness while he watched the people.

To one end of the room, grouped around the fire, were the workmen, drinking quietly together, their faces serious and anxious; they seemed to be listening to someone, probably Banim, the foreman. Along the walls of the pub were the townspeople; the professions – doctor, teacher, clergy – sitting together, sharing a private joke, although they kept glancing across at the workmen. And then there were the shopkeepers and the farmers, some of the latter still in their working clothes and boots, with the women sitting quietly at one table, heads close together.

In a town like this everyone had their place – and knew it. In the pub only he was the outsider.

Michael turned around and caught the barman's eye. 'Old Matt,' he asked, 'is he in tonight?'

The barman looked hard at him for a few minutes and then jerked his head towards the fire and the group of workmen before turning away.

Michael eased his way through the crowd towards the fireplace and, as he neared, he could hear a soft voice, cracked with age, droning on. 'And then of course there was that time in Galway when a local man, an O'Grady I think it was, uprooted one of *their* trees. Well, no sooner had he done so when a terrible wailing and crying started up, and the sap on the tree turned bright red and flowed like blood, and the branches twisted and formed themselves into limbs until the whole tree took on the likeness of a young woman. It may be there still.' The voice paused and then added in a different tone, 'Of course O'Grady isn't; it doesn't do to interfere with the faeries.'

'What will happen then if the mound is flattened?' Michael asked suddenly.

There was a long moment's silence in which all heads turned in his direction. Old Matt settled back into his chair by the fire and lifted his half-finished pint from the table. He sipped from it and then shrugged his bony shoulders. 'I don't know,' he confessed. 'I believe however, that the Faerie Host might come out,' he added with a wry smile.

'And then again, they might not,' Michael said quietly.

The old man shrugged again. 'They might not,' he agreed, 'but I would certainly not like to put it to the test.'

Heads nodded in agreement as Michael looked around the group. 'Do you know that Weiss has threatened to bring in his own men to finish the job,' he said into the silence.

'It's their funeral,' someone said from near the bar.

Michael spun around. 'No, it's *your* funeral. This plant can put the town on the map, and bring in a lot of money ... *if* you cooperate. But if word gets out that you were not willing to honour your contracts and finish the construction ...' He trailed off, looking at the blank, shut faces; he just wasn't getting through to them.

'The Faerie Host rode out in my grandmother's time,' Matt said quietly. 'One of them claimed a human bride but was then forced to return her when the girl's husband came looking for her. Not long after that a young girl was found dead at the foot of the mound on the morning after All Hallows' Eve, and there was another time when my grandmother told me that she had been blessed by the faerie folk for a great service that she had done them.'* The pub had gone deathly silent, the only sound the hissing of the fire and the distant sound of wind and rain. 'And although my grandmother was a poor woman and had lived here nearly all her life,' Matt continued, 'she died wealthy ... a very wealthy woman indeed.' The old man finished his drink and continued quickly. 'They *are* there, the faerie folk, charming and delightful when they want to be, dangerous and capricious at will. They have slept for a generation, let them sleep in peace,' he begged.

Michael shook his head. 'There's nothing I can do. If it was my decision ...' he shrugged, 'but it's not.'

'But you can talk to your office, explain the situation ...'

'I already have; the project is to go ahead.'

A short burly man stood up from his seat beside the fire. 'If the American brings in his own men they'll get no cooperation from anyone in the town: there'll be no lodgings, no shop will sell them food and no pub will serve them drink. We can make it hard for them.'

'Mr Banim,' Michael said quietly, 'you're a small country

---

* see 'The Magic Lingers On' ... 'Into the Shadowland' ... 'Into Eternity' ... *Irish Folk & Fairy Tales vol. 1*

town; you cannot go against the Irish Government and a large American corporation. They have both invested a lot of money in this project, and they are not going to stand by and see it wasted.'

'If they flatten the mound,' Matt said in a voice that was little more than a whisper, 'they may not have any choice.'

From the window of his hotel room Weiss could see the fields and the rusting machinery over the roofs of the cottages. A thin moon slipped from between the racing clouds, touching the metal with silver and coating the crest of the low mound in harsh reflective light.

Rain patterned against the window, and the small American absently rubbed his hand across the misted glass and squinted down into the rain-washed street. For a brief moment he found himself wondering what this town must have looked like a hundred years ago; similar to countless small country towns all across Europe, he should imagine; similar to the town from which his grandparents would have emigrated to the States.

He wiped down the glass again and looked across at the mound. He had spent the day in Dublin, checking through the countless volumes of folklore, myth and legend in the libraries and bookshops ... and he had come away more than a little disturbed.

He had come away with the knowledge that in no other country in Europe was the faerie tradition so strongly maintained and believed in by the country people. He had read some of the folklore collected by people like Hyde, Yeats, Lady Gregory, O'Sullivan and many, many more. And if one single fact stood out in the vast wealth of material that was available, it was the belief – the firmly held belief – that the faeries, the *gentry*, the leprechaun, the Shining Ones, the *ban* and *mna shee* existed.

Clouds closed in and the moonlight abruptly vanished,

plunging the countryside into darkness . . . and that terrified Weiss. Born and reared in the heart of the city that never sleeps, he had never really known total darkness until this trip to Ireland. Beyond the town there was nothing, no lights – except the dim and distant beams of a car's headlights, and they only served somehow to intensify the darkness – no sound, except the soughing of the wind – the loneliest sound in the world.

With the light gone, there was only his own reflection in the glass, and he turned away. On the table beside his bed a couple of empty bottles lay side by side with those which had yet to be drunk. Weiss used a bottle-opener and prised the top off one and began to drink straight from the bottle. He flopped down on the hard bed and continued drinking; there was precious little else to do in this God-forsaken hole of a town.

He awoke much later that night, lying flat out across the bed, still fully dressed. The air in the room was close and heavy with the odours of stale sweat, spilled drink . . . and something else. Weiss lay there, slowly becoming aware of the sudden chill in the room and the brightness outside his window. He sat up slowly, his heart beginning to pound and cold perspiration slowly trickling down his neck. His hand was trembling as he reached for the bedside light, but when he flicked the switch nothing happened.

A shadow moved across the window: tall and thin, with two hard points of green-gold light where the eyes should be. Weiss froze, the pounding of his heart increasing rapidly and painfully. He pushed his way up on the bed until his back touched the headboard and he drew his knees up to his chin. He tried to speak, but no sound came out.

The shadow-figure glided closer to the bed, the moonlight streaming through the window giving it both shape and definition. It was a man, excessively tall and thin as he had already noticed, and the moonlight touched his long, slightly Asiatic face with silver, with the shadows accentuating the high cheekbones, the pointed chin, the sharply tipped ears. And his eyes were like polished emeralds. They bored through the crouching American, stripping bare his soul, seeking the undersized Brooklyn urchin that still hid beneath the bluster.

Weiss didn't know how long the tableau lasted, but then the figure smiled, his teeth startlingly white against the shadow of his face, and the American buried his head in his arms and prayed, for the first time in over three decades, to a God he thought he had forgotten.


When he awoke the sun was streaming in through the window, a long bar of harsh light lying warmly across his face. He groaned and rolled over, allowing his senses time to reorientate themselves ... and came shockingly alert. His dream of the previous night returned vividly – or was it a dream? He could remember every detail with vivid clarity; surely it had been too real, too frightening to be a dream.

And all his dreams had died in his youth.

He examined the locks on the doors, but they were intact and didn't seem to have been tampered with. The window was painted shut, and the room adjoining his – a tiny bathroom – was windowless. Of course, it could have been one of the townspeople trying to frighten him, he reasoned. He checked the walls, tapping for any hollow spots, but they all seemed solid enough, and the ceiling was covered with squares of white tiling. Therefore no one could have entered the room, and it must have been a dream; there was no other reasonable explanation.

And Carl Weiss was not even prepared to consider any other explanations.


The new workers began arriving in the small town around noon. They were city men, mainly from Dublin and Belfast, with a few from Cork and Waterford, and their foreman was a short, stocky Londoner. The townspeople watched their arrival in silence, and waited until the buses departed, leaving the men standing in sullen silence, and then one by one they turned away, leaving the outsiders alone on the broad, windswept street.

Michael Hughes watched them from his bedroom window. He had just come from a long talk with Banim, in a last ditch attempt to try and have the work go ahead, but the foreman was adamant: his men would not touch the mound.

Weiss appeared below. He seemed more than a little drunk, his normally florid face was flushed and his eyes were protruding. He conversed with the new workers for a few moments, his arms moving wildly, and when he was finished the men raised a ragged cheer, before turning and tramping off towards the fields.

Shortly afterwards the sound of engines rent the quiet country air, and a cloud of dust rose up and quickly blanketed the fields. The noise and activity continued until darkness fell and then scores of camp fires blossomed up, studding the fields with shivering lights – and also answering one of Michael's questions: where was Weiss going to lodge the workers. Michael grinned slightly; it was a cold, damp field, and promised to be a wet and windy night, and he certainly wouldn't care to be spending a night under canvas.

Michael wandered down from his room close to midnight. He couldn't sleep, there was something in the air, something like a brewing storm, a tenseness ... an expectancy. He walked slowly down the cold, damp streets, his leather soled shoes echoing hollowly off the old stone walls. On more than one occasion he saw the curtains twitch or a shadow move behind the windows; it seemed he was not the only one who could not sleep that night. Almost unconsciously he found himself walking in the direction of the camp. There had been singing and shouting earlier on that evening, but the only sounds now on the night air were the crackled settlings of the many camp fires and the ghostly whistling of the wind ... and that too was strange, for they were the *only* sounds. He stood still and listened; no night birds called, nothing rustled through the grass ... silence.

He kept close to the hedges at the edge of the field and made his way towards the fort. There was a crescent-shaped moon high in the heavens, surrounded by a ghostly nimbus of cloud, shedding a delicate illumination over everything. Every now and again it would disappear behind a thick black cloud, but these were few and far between, and Michael had a torch tucked into his pocket. When he reached the edge of the field the moon disappeared briefly, and he stood quietly watching the silver move slowly behind the cloud, and then gracefully reappear again.

Although he had been expecting it, it was still something of a shock to discover the damage the diggers had done to the mound. Most of the field around it had been torn up and the side closest to him had been gouged out, and it gaped like a dark, open wound. At this rate they would have the entire fort flattened by noon tomorrow.

Michael took a step forward – and then something struck him across the base of the spine, sending him sprawling into the mire. A booted foot came down inches from his face and a hard hand gripped his hair and pulled his head back.

'Well, what have we got here?' The voice was flat and heavy with a Dublin accent.

Michael was yanked to his feet, his arm twisted painfully behind his back, forcing him up onto his toes. 'Put me down ... what 'n hell's going on?' he demanded.

'Well Mr Hughes, I must admit I never expected to find you here.' A torch snapped on, blinding him, and then flicked off again. When the orange spots on his retina disappeared, he found he could make out Carl Weiss and another worker standing before him. The American nodded at the Dubliner holding Michael. 'Let him go ... but make sure Mr Hughes doesn't try to go anywhere,' he added. 'I must admit,' he continued thoughtfully, 'I had rather imagined that you would send some of your friends along to do your dirty work for you ...'

'What are you talking about?' Michael snapped. His spine was throbbing and the ribs in his lower back ached; he would bring charges for assault.

The small American smiled, his face bone-white in the moonlight, his teeth alabaster chips against the dark hollow of his mouth. 'Come now Mr Hughes, let's not play the innocent. Do you deny that you came here tonight with the intention of sabotaging some of our equipment, and then laying the blame on the ... faeries?' His voice was heavy with sarcasm, and tinged with something else which Michael couldn't identify.

'You forget, Mr Hughes,' he continued drily, 'I am American, and in the States we do things differently ... and that includes protecting our investment.' He nodded at the two burly guards. 'There are men staked out all around this camp,' he announced proudly, 'and as soon as any of your friends come near the machinery or the mound, well...' He let the sentence hang.

'What will we do with him?' the Dubliner asked suddenly.

Weiss stared at Michael for a long time, and the young man suddenly felt his blood run cold, for the small, soft American, ridiculous in his three-piece suit and rubber boots was gone, and in his place stood a small and dangerous animal, with sharp, pitiless eyes and a scavenger's grin.

'I think Mr Hughes deserves to be taught a lesson,' the American whispered, his lips smiling, but his eyes remaining hard and cold. 'It will also show our village friends that we mean business ... and who knows, perhaps they'll reconsider their foolish decision to shun us.' Weiss turned away. 'He's all yours,' he said quietly to the two workers.

Michael managed to cry out once, and then an open hand cracked across his face, numbing him with shock rather than pain, and he was too stunned even to resist as his other arm was now hauled up behind his back and twisted savagely.

Time was a human measurement and the elven folk did not number the passing days and keep the fleeting years. If anything of theirs reckoned time, it was a subtle appreciation of nature, of spans of growth, decay and regrowth ... for there was no death in the elven fields.

And yet if they did measure time as humans did, it might be said that they had rested in their hidden world for many years without appearing and walking the fields of man. The last time they had sallied forth had been ... when? One human generation ago? Two? More?

But the humans did not bother them and they, in turn, did not interfere with the sons of man. Occasionally they felt the fleeting touches of human emotions: fear, wonder, awe and sometimes amusement as someone walked the mound.

But lately there had been a great disturbance, both mental and physical. Many, many humans walked the fields above their heads, and the very soil itself was racked with pain.

And now the fort itself was under attack.

The descendants of the Tuatha De Danann had felt with an almost personal and physical pain the huge mechanical diggers ripping into the sides of the mound. They knew that even if the entire mound was levelled to the ground they would still survive, but the mound was a link with the fields of man, one of the last links ...

The Faerie Host rode forth.

Michael's head exploded in pain, lights flaring behind his

eyes, and his ears began to throb painfully. He cried aloud, his mind shouting pain, before his senses registered that he had not, in fact, been struck. He heard a shout and then another, and then he was suddenly thrown to the ground, and he heard booted feet running across the soft earth.

Michael sat up stiffly, his eyes blinking wide in astonishment, for the night was bright with a soft glowing light. It was softer than moonlight and yet stronger, and flowed from the ripped-out side of the faerie fort, gathering into a pale glowing fog that drifted across the fields swathing everything within its folds. He cringed as the thick white blanket slowly enfolded him. It was surprisingly warm and dry, not cold and wet, and carried with it the odours of strange herbs and spices. Sounds became muffled, and the shouts of fear and anger were quickly dulled and then lost within it, and the air became leaden and still. There was silence for what seemed like a long time, and then haunting notes drifted through the night, snatches of old songs, whispers and tendrils of music hung on the air as if they could be touched.

Michael felt a longing well up deep inside him; a desire, an overpowering, overwhelming desire for ... what? He didn't know. He brushed away the sudden sting of tears with the back of his hand. He felt as if he had lost something ... something ... something ...

And he never realised that he wept for his youth, his lost innocence.

Shadows moved through the fog; tall, thin creatures that strode purposefully past him, metal clinking and jangling as they moved, and once he thought he heard a horse whinny.

Slowly, his back and spine throbbing painfully, Michael eased himself to his feet and began to walk towards the mound and the source of the light. He discovered then that there was a slight breeze blowing away from the mound, a warm, scented breeze that somehow reminded him of the long hot summers of his youth. The musical notes were more audible now; they hung sweet and clear like no other tune he had ever heard. And then there was a single note, a clarion call. He heard a rhythmic jangling and a steady throbbing beat coupled with a metallic tingling on the air. He stood indecisively, listening to it rapidly approaching him ... and then he abruptly realised what he was hearing.

Michael threw himself to one side as the Faerie Host rode back into the fields of man. A flailing hoof caught the sole of his shoe, and the blow jarred his leg all the way up to his hip: these were no ghosts, no shadows! He had a momentary glimpse of tall, thin proud figures clad in fantastic garb, riding mounts that were equally strange, before the glowing fog closed in again – and the screaming started.


He was lying on his back in the middle of the field when he awoke. He was shivering violently and his clothes were sodden with dew. He attempted to rise, and then groaned aloud as his stiff joints and muscles protested and the pain in the small of his back and twisted shoulders made itself felt.

The morning was silent; no birds sang, no creatures moved through the grass, no wind disturbed the trees ... and he experienced the same feeling he had the night before – one of expectancy about the place. He found he was alone in the field, there was no sign of the new workers, their camp or Weiss ... even the traces of the camp fires had vanished. Michael came slowly to his feet and limped painfully across the field towards the mound. Mist still clung to its sides, and it swirled and coiled about him as he moved into it, shifting and weaving like a nest of serpents.

And when he reached the side of the fort he found it was whole again!

There was no trace of the gaping hole where the mechanical diggers had torn out the side, no flattened grass,

208

scarred with heavy track and tyre marks.

There was a figure sitting atop the mound wrapped in a long silver-edged green cloak. He turned his head and gestured with one long thin hand, calling Michael up.

The young man hauled himself up the side of the fort, slipping and sliding on the dew-damp grass, while the stranger merely sat there, staring out across the fields, neither looking at him, nor making any effort to help. There was an air of complete detachment about him, and as Michael neared him, he began to make out the differences in the stranger.

Although he was sitting cross-legged and partially enveloped in the long cloak, Michael's first impression was of height coupled with extreme thinness. His head seemed almost misshapen; high cheekbones and a pronounced suborbital ridge gave his eyes a sunken appearance. His chin protruded and came to a point, and his ears were set close to his head and pointed also and tipped with tufts of fine black hair that matched the hair on his head.

'Who ... who are you?' Michael panted.

The young man's eyes flicked across at him and then turned back to his surveillance of the fields. Michael sat down beside him, drawing his legs up to his chin and resting his pounding head on them. A fit of shivering took him, leaving him exhausted.

'My name is Aran,' the stranger said suddenly, his voice – crystal clear and almost vibrant – startling Michael.

'Michael,' he introduced himself.

'I know.' Again that disquieting flick of the eyes before they turned back to the fields.

'What happened last night?' Michael asked eventually, when the youth made no move to say anything else.

'We rode.'

'We?'

The young man stood suddenly, unfolding himself with a

fluid grace; Michael eased himself to his feet, groaning aloud, and he found that Aran stood a head and more taller than him.

'Blood called us, and then we felt the disturbance,' the elven lord said, 'and the Host rode against the threat.'

Michael nodded. 'I see; what happened to the men?'

'They sleep in drunken slumber beyond the town; in the main they are unharmed, but they will never return to this place.'

'And the townsfolk?'

'They heard shouting and cries during the night, but they will assume it was a drunken brawl ... some of course will know, but they will say nothing.'

'And Weiss?' Michael asked finally.

But Aran only smiled and nodded towards the east. 'The sun rises, I cannot linger.' He started to walk down the side of the mound.

'Wait ... wait ...' Michael shook his head to clear it. He must be feverish, he had to be dreaming this. He slid down the side of the fort and came to a stop before the tall figure. 'Are you real?' he whispered.

Aran smiled, his teeth very pale and pointed. 'What do you think?'

'You look real ... but, faeries don't exist,' he finished in a rush.

'No, I suppose they don't,' Aran agreed.

'Then what are you?' Michael demanded.

'What do the country people call us?'

'The Shining Ones, the Sidhe, the Tuatha De Danann ...'

Aran nodded. 'And that is what we are. The last of the Tuatha De Danann, the People of the Goddess. We continue to exist because the people continue to believe in us. We are also tied to this land, and this is the last outpost of Faerie in this world. It will be a sadder, poorer place when we are gone – and that day is drawing ever closer.' The elven lord looked down on the young man. 'I am the last born of my race; born of a human mother and elven sire, mine was the first birth for many, many years. The elven race is dying, son of Man.'

'But ... but, what do you need to survive?'

'Faith!' And the elven lord walked down the side of the fort into the swirling mist, and was gone.

And Michael Hughes stood on the side of the mound and watched the sun rise over the last outpost of Faerie.


*'Work on the Irish American project has been called off, it was announced last night. A re-evaluation of the costs involved, coupled with rising prices and spiralling inflation in Ireland, has caused the American backers to pull out and work on the project has stopped.*

*'Meanwhile, a verdict of accidental death has been returned in the case of Carl Weiss, the overseer of the project. Mr Weiss was found drowned in a river which runs close to the site of the projected plant. Mr Weiss, it is reported, suffered a massive heart attack.'*

# Author's Note

The stories in this, and the two previous collections, were collected during the summers of 1977, '78 and '79, along the south and west coast of Ireland, where the story-telling tradition is still very strong. And while I have, in many cases, changed, altered or otherwise interfered with the outline of the story, the core remains untouched and, I would hope, in the *'tradition'*.

As a postscript to this collection, in the late summer of 1982 workers in the De Lorean car plant in Northern Ireland claimed that one of the reasons the business ran into so much trouble was because a fairy thorn bush had been disturbed during the construction of the plant. Apparently the management took this so seriously that they actually had a similar bush brought in and planted with all due ceremony!

Michael Scott

Suggested Further Reading:

| Colum, Padraig: | A Treasury of Irish Folklore. | 1954 |
|---|---|---|
| Curtin, Jeremiah: | Myths and Folklore of Ireland. | 1890 |
| Gregory, Lady: | Cuchulain of Muirthemne. | 1902 & 1970 |
| | Gods and Fighting Men. | 1904 & 1970 |
| | Visions and Beliefs in the West of Ireland. | 1920 & 1970 |
| Hyde, Douglas: | Legends of Saints and Sinners. | 1915 |
| | Beside the Fire. | 1910 & 1978 |
| Jacobs, Joseph: | Celtic Fairy Tales & More Celtic Fairy Tales. | 1894 & 1968 |
| Joyce, P.W.: | Old Celtic Romances. | 1879 & 1977 |
| O'Faolain, Eileen: | Irish Sagas and Folktales. | 1954 |
| | Children of the Salmon. | 1965 |
| O'Sullivan, Sean: | The Folklore of Ireland. | 1974 |
| | Folktales of Ireland. | 1966 |
| Wilde, Lady: | Ancient Legends of Ireland. | 1888 & 1971 |
| Yeats, W.B.: | Fairy and Folktales of the Irish Peasantry. | 1888 |
| | Irish Fairy Tales. | 1892 |
| | together as Fairy and Folktales of Ireland. | 1973 |

This short list merely points the way towards some of the vast wealth of material that is available on Irish Folklore. But there is still a lot of material that has not been collected – indeed, many of the stories in Irish Folk and Fairy Tales volumes I, II and III have never before appeared in print.

# A SELECTION OF BESTSELLERS FROM SPHERE

**FICTION**

| | | |
|---|---|---|
| THE MISTS OF AVALON | Marion Bradley | £2.95 ☐ |
| THE INNOCENT DARK | J. S. Forrester | £1.95 ☐ |
| THURSTON HOUSE | Danielle Steel | £1.95 ☐ |
| MAIDEN VOYAGE | Graham Masterton | £2.50 ☐ |
| THE FURTHER ADVENTURES OF | | |
| HUCKLEBERRY FINN | Greg Matthews | £2.95 ☐ |

**FILM AND TV TIE-INS**

| | | |
|---|---|---|
| THE IRISH R.M. | E. E. Somerville and | |
| | Martin Ross | £1.95 ☐ |
| SCARFACE | Paul Monette | £1.75 ☐ |
| THE KILLING OF KAREN SILKWOOD | | |
| | Richard Rashke | £1.95 ☐ |
| THE RADISH DAY JUBILEE | Sheilah B. Bruce | £1.50 ☐ |
| THEY CALL ME BOOBER FRAGGLE | | |
| | Michaela Muntean | £1.50 ☐ |
| RED AND THE PUMPKINS | Jocelyn Stevenson | £1.50 ☐ |

**NON-FICTION**

| | | |
|---|---|---|
| GRENADA: INVASION, REVOLUTION | | |
| AND AFTERMATH | Hugh O'Shaughnessy | £2.95 ☐ |
| DIETING MAKES YOU FAT | Geoffrey Cannon & | |
| | Hetty Einzig | £1.95 ☐ |
| THE FRUIT AND NUT BOOK | Helena Radecka | £6.95 ☐ |
| LEBANON, THE FRACTURED COUNTRY | | |
| | David Gilmour | £2.95 ☐ |
| THE OFFICIAL MARTIAL ARTS HANDBOOK | | |
| | David Mitchell | £3.95 ☐ |

*All Sphere books are available at your local bookshop or newsagent, or can be ordered direct from the publisher. Just tick the titles you want and fill in the form below.*

Name _____

Address _____

_____

Write to Sphere Books, Cash Sales Department, P.O. Box 11, Falmouth, Cornwall TR10 9EN

Please enclose a cheque or postal order to the value of the cover price plus:

UK: 45p for the first book, 20p for the second book and 14p for each additional book ordered to a maximum charge of £1.63.

OVERSEAS: 75p for the first book and 21p per copy for each additional book.

BFPO & EIRE: 45p for the first book, 20p for the second book plus 14p per copy for the next 7 books, thereafter 8p per book.

*Sphere Books reserve the right to show new retail prices on covers which may differ from those previously advertised in the text or elsewhere, and to increase postal rates in accordance with the PO.*